The exciting conclusion
It began with OUTP
mysterious relic in a bl
the Antarctic ice...

It continued with A.
Bones joining forces with Jade Ihara and Nick
Kismet to find more of the Elementals--four
powerful artifacts, older than civilization itself.

Now, in MAGUS, the heroic team--
accompanied by Maddock's old friends Professor
and Jimmy Letson, will search the last Elemental
relic--the Emerald Tablet, hidden away in the tomb
of history's most legendary conqueror.

But they aren't the only ones looking for it.
Agents of Prometheus, a mysterious secret society,
are also searching for the relics, intent on using their
awesome power to rule the world.

PRAISE FOR DAVID WOOD AND THE DANE MADDOCK ADVENTURES!

A great read that provides lots of action, and
thoughtful insight as well, into strange realms that
are sometimes best left unexplored." *Paul
Kemprecos, author of Cool Blue Tomb*

"David Wood has done it again. Quest takes you
on an expedition that leads down a trail of
adventure and thrills!" *David L. Golemon, Author of
the Event Group series*

MAGUS

A DANE MADDOCK ADVENTURE

DAVID WOOD
SEAN ELLIS

MAGUS
Copyright 2018 by David Wood
All rights reserved

Published by Adrenaline Press
www.adrenaline.press

Adrenaline Press is an imprint of Gryphonwood Press
www.gryphonwoodpress.com

ISBN-13: 978-1-940095-98-1
ISBN-10: 1-940095-98-0

BOOKS and SERIES by DAVID WOOD

The Dane Maddock Adventures
Dourado
Cibola
Quest
Icefall
Buccaneer
Atlantis
Ark
Xibalba
Loch
Solomon Key

Dane and Bones Origins
Freedom
Hell Ship
Splashdown
Dead Ice
Liberty
Electra
Amber
Justice
Treasure of the Dead

Adventures from the Dane Maddock Universe
Destination-Rio
Destination-Luxor
Berserk
The Tomb
Devil's Face
Outpost

Arcanum
Magus
Brainwash
Herald
Maug
Cavern

Jade Ihara Adventures (with Sean Ellis)
Oracle
Changeling
Exile

Bones Bonebrake Adventures
Primitive
The Book of Bones
Skin and Bones
Venom

Jake Crowley Adventures (with Alan Baxter)
Blood Codex
Anubis Key

Brock Stone Adventures
Arena of Souls
Track of the Beast (forthcoming)

Myrmidon Files (with Sean Ellis)
Destiny
Mystic

Sam Aston Investigations (with Alan Baxter)
Primordial
Overlord

Stand-Alone Novels
Into the Woods (with David S. Wood)
Callsign: Queen (with Jeremy Robinson)
Dark Rite (with Alan Baxter)

David Wood writing as David Debord

The Absent Gods Trilogy
The Silver Serpent
Keeper of the Mists
The Gates of Iron

The Impostor Prince (with Ryan A. Span)
Neptune's Key
The Zombie-Driven Life
You Suck

BOOKS and SERIES by SEAN ELLIS

The Nick Kismet Adventures
The Shroud of Heaven
Into the Black
The Devil You Know (Novella)
Fortune Favors

The Adventures of Dodge Dalton
In the Shadow of Falcon's Wings
At the Outpost of Fate
On the High Road to Oblivion
Against the Fall of Eternal Night (with Kerry Frey)

PART ONE: HELL WEEK

Prologue

It is a perfect storm.

Hour after hour, a total assault on the senses. Artillery simulators and machine guns firing blanks nonstop, the noise crackling through my nerves like lightning. Smoke grenades spewing out a putrid fume. The stink of body odor. The scrape of sand on skin already rubbed raw and bloody. Running down to the tideline where the cold waves wash over me, sapping my strength until I've got nothing left to give.

The worst part though is that voice. A low flat monotone, barely distinguishable from the pounding surf. I wouldn't be able to hear it at all if not for the amplification of the bullhorn, but it resonates through me, dragging me molecule by molecule into a black pit of despair, sucking away what's left of my resolve.

"You don't have to keep doing this," the voice drones.

And I know he's right.

"You can go get in my truck right now. I've got some hot cocoa for you. That sounds good, doesn't it? Come ring my bell and you can have some."

There are a few defiant shouts. "Hell no, chief."

My voice is not among them. Even if I wanted to, I don't think I could get the words past my chattering teeth.

The voice drones on for a while, alternately elaborating on the effects of hypothermia and then, with something that sounds almost like sympathy, offering absolution. "Not everyone is cut out for this. This is what we do, every day... Is this what you really want? To be miserable all the time? Hot cocoa in the truck... All you have to do is ring my bell."

Is this what I really want? I can't remember why I ever thought it was.

"Boat crews," the voice says abruptly. "Line up."

I look left then right, seeing the others. Our arms are linked but we might as well be on different planets. As another wave crashes over my head, I see some of the others responding. Thrashing in the surf, struggling to rise. Struggling to help each other.

Then I'm moving, too.

We all stumble up onto the beach, assembling into our six-man boat crews, only none of the boat crews are complete. How many are left? I can't tell. There had been seventy-two of us at the start, but more than a dozen folded in the first hour.

How long ago was that? I can't remember.

"You look tired," drones the instructor as he paces up and down the line. Viewed in profile, the bullhorn looks like a part of him, a strange deformed animal muzzle, braying constantly. "Maybe you should all lie down."

A groan <u>ripples</u> through the rank; we all know

what's coming.

I drop to my back with everyone else and immediately begin kicking. Flutter kicks. God, I hate flutter kicks. My abdominal muscles scream in protest.

The instructor counts out the rhythm for a while—"One, two, three..." We are expected to keep the count, sounding off at the top of our lungs, but the only sound I can make is a mewling grunt. Then the instructor breaks off to ask, "How was the water? Did you enjoy your swim?"

A ragged chorus of "Hooyah, chief," goes up.

"I'll bet you'd really like to get back out there, wouldn't you?"

"Hooyah, chief."

"On your feet."

I'm supposed to bound up, but it feels like I'm trapped in quicksand. Every muscle screams in protest.

"What's this?" the instructor says, his voice rising ever so slightly, a mockery of sincere interest. "I thought there were supposed to be six men to a boat crew." He looks over to one of the other instructors, who nods, right on cue. The chief shakes his head. "Some of these boat crews are light. Looks like we're going to have to change things up a little." He paces up and down the line for a few minutes. "Well this is a little awkward. I count fifty-six maggots lined up in front of me."

The instructor stops abruptly—

No. Not me. Don't look at me. Keep going.

—and looks right at me. "Maggot, how many times does six go into fifty-six?"

My teeth are chattering involuntarily, but some part of my brain has already done the math. "Nine, chief. Remainder of two."

I've always been good at math. I'm good at almost everything.

Except this.

Another voice, one that I've come to despise over the last two weeks, snarls from somewhere off to my right. "Teacher's pet."

It's the big Indian, though in this moment, I can't remember his name. I can barely remember my own.

"Remainder of two," *croons the instructor.* "Well that makes this easy. As soon as two of you maggots ring my bell, we can move on with the next activity."

He pauses, allowing this to sink in. "You already know that you're not going to make it," *he continues, easing back into the monotone.* "You know that you're going to quit. Why put yourself through this?"

I know that some of them are already considering it because I am, but none of us break ranks.

"No one?" *The instructor feigns disappointment.* "All right then. Go for a swim and think it over."

I groan. I think about stumbling out into the surf again, and I think about doing that over and over and over... And then I think about what it would be like to just take that step in the other direction. End the nightmare. It would be so simple….

"Jimmy, don't!"

The shout snaps me back into the moment. I look around and see a young man from one of the other boat crews shambling forward. Until this moment, I didn't know his name—he's maggot, just like me, just like everyone else—but I know his face to the extent that I know any of them.

But in a minute or two, he'll be gone like he never even existed.

The same voice of protest sounds again. "Jimmy! Come on, buddy. We're in this together, remember? We promised each other we'd finish it together."

Jimmy's friend I do recognize. It's the young junior lieutenant, the one the Indian calls… What was it, again?

Pope.

Pope Maddock.

Jimmy just shakes his head. "I can't, Dane… Can't do it."

I see the hollow look on Jimmy's face as he turns away, and I know that, no matter what promises he made, he's done.

"I quit," *Jimmy mumbles, and staggers toward the chief.*

I quit.

The words strike against something in my core, like steel striking flint, and then I'm moving, heading down toward the surf again.

Because I won't quit, no matter what. And whenever I think about ringing the bell, I see his face, and it reminds me that I'm not him....

1.

Annapolis, Maryland

Pete "Professor" Chapman blinked and let the memory slip away, bringing his attention fully into the present as James "Jimmy" Letson, walked right by him, showing not even a hint of recognition, and exited the hotel lobby. Professor, seated at a corner table in the continental breakfast dining room and pretending to read the morning edition of the Washington Post, watched him for a few seconds longer, before tucking the newspaper under one arm and rising to follow.

The face Professor remembered so well looked different now. Older, the cheeks fuller, rounder. Softened by too much junk food and booze, and not enough exercise. He supposed that was to be expected. They had all been young men back then, some not even old enough to drink legally.

That face—the face of the quitter—had been an anchor for him. A lifeline that had gotten him through what he thought would be the worst four days of his life.

The Navy called it BUD/S—Basic Underwater Demolition/SEAL training—phase one. Unofficially, it was just called Hell Week. It was the final exercise of the three-week introductory evolution of BUD/S in which candidates were subjected to a rigorous ordeal of physical exertion and sleep deprivation with just one goal: to identify those with the physical and mental toughness to become Navy SEALs. Four days in which candidates were put through the grinder—pushed to exhaustion, denied sleep, subjected to constant harassment. The attrition rate for the exercise was always high—typically in the neighborhood of eighty percent—and Professor's class had been no different.

There was no secret to surviving Hell Week. The purpose of the exercise was to strip away the ego completely, revealing whatever lay underneath. You either had that toughness or you didn't. Professor had found it that morning when he'd watched Jimmy Letson drop out. Over the course of the next three days, whenever he felt like he had nothing left to give, he would mutter, like a mantra, "I'm not Jimmy."

After it was over, after he survived and advanced to the next phase of SEAL training, he had let all memory of that face slip away, and would have forgotten Jimmy completely if not for the fact that his platoon leader, Lt. Dane Maddock, had remained friends with Jimmy Letson.

Now, seeing that face again after nearly twenty-five years, Professor felt the old emotions rising unbidden.

Jimmy, the quitter.

He was surprised and a little dismayed at the

vehemence he felt. Lots of guys washed out. For every sailor who earned his Budweiser—the distinctive eagle-trident-pistol badge of the SEALs—there were four or more hopefuls who rang the bell during Hell Week. They weren't inherently weak or flawed. Every single one of them was still among that brave minority who had taken an oath to defend America. It was profoundly unfair to call any of them quitters, and in truth, Professor never had.

Except for Jimmy.

Twenty-two hours earlier, when Tam Broderick gave him this assignment, the only context in which he thought of Jimmy was as Dane's friend. The reporter. The researcher. The hacker.

After washing out of BUDS, Letson had taken an assignment with Navy public affairs, finishing his term of service as a Navy journalist, after which he had gone back to school to become a journalist, and had gone on to have a very successful career as an investigative reporter, thanks in no small part to his online prowess. A true child of the digital age, Jimmy Letson had been a computer hacker before there was even a word for it. A lifelong tech geek, he built his own hardware and wrote his own code. As far as Professor knew, Jimmy wasn't a Black Hat, using his skills to defraud or sow the seeds of anarchy. Instead, he was a sort of cyber-muckraker and champion of the fifth estate, while sometimes moonlighting as a researcher for Dane Maddock, who was now a private citizen and a professional treasure hunter.

It was this latter association that had brought him once more into Professor's orbit. Maddock and his crew had occasionally done some freelance work of their own for Tam Broderick as part of her task force dedicated to battling the quasi-religious far-right criminal conspiracy known as "the Dominion." Jimmy Letson had not been a part of that arrangement—indeed, while they were aware of each other, to the best of Professor's knowledge, Tam and Jimmy had never met, but nonetheless shared a deep mutual distrust.

Evidently, Tam's distrust extended to maintaining surreptitious electronic surveillance on Jimmy, which was how she came to notice that something was very much amiss in Letson's world. Without any warning, Jimmy Letson had vanished, disappearing both from his physical life and from his considerable online presence.

The disappearance was alarming enough to prompt Tam to pull Professor off his current long-term assignment, as bodyguard for archaeologist Jade Ihara, who just happened to be a former paramour of Dane Maddock. Professor had left her in Cuzco, Peru, where she was running down some kind of mystery related to an old occult manuscript, and embarked on the fourteen-hour flight Washington D.C. where it had taken him all of four hours to locate Jimmy Letson, who was currently using the alias Ryan Duarte, and staying in a hotel in Annapolis, Maryland.

Letson went straight to his rental car—a red

Hyundai Sonata—in the parking lot. Professor loitered near the hotel entrance waiting until Jimmy had pulled out onto the street, before hurrying to his own rental—a silver Toyota Prius—to take up the pursuit. He didn't need to worry about losing Jimmy in traffic; he'd tagged the Sonata with an RFID tracking chip.

Professor had tracked Jimmy down without much difficulty, which frankly surprised him. Given the man's reputation as a hacker-extraordinaire, he had expected Jimmy to do a much better job covering his tracks. It was enough to make Professor wonder if he wasn't being played. Maybe Jimmy was on a fishing expedition, trying to lure him or someone like him into the open.

But the reporter-cum-hacker was exhibiting none of the tells of a seasoned professional; no casual glances to check for surveillance as he left the hotel, no sudden turns on the road to check for a tail. Jimmy drove like any other commuter, moving along with the flow of traffic for a couple miles before turning onto Maryland Route 178—Generals Highway—heading west. He continued on for several miles before merging onto the I-97, still heading west, but instead of following the Interstate north toward Baltimore, or turning south toward D.C. he kept going west.

Tam's assumption was that Jimmy had stirred up some kind of hornet's nest and gone into hiding. Professor wasn't so sure. His sense was that Jimmy was neither running nor hiding, but chasing something. Or more likely someone. A government whistleblower, perhaps, someone living in the sprawling suburban hinterland surrounding the nation's capital.

Perplexed, and more than a little alarmed, Professor sped up, closing with his quarry until only a couple cars separated them. As Jimmy continued down the freeway skirting the southern edge of Fort George Meade, Professor became even more certain, not only of his read on Jimmy's general intention but also the reporter's current destination. He wasn't at all surprised when the Sonata turned off at the Canine Road exit, just south of Annapolis Junction, and drove into the visitor's parking lot at the entrance to the sprawling campus of the National Security Agency.

"What are you up to, Letson?" Professor muttered.

2.

The man calling himself Ryan Duarte presented a government-issued CAC—Common Access Card— to the guard at the visitor control center, and waited patiently for the computerized card reader to confirm that he was authorized to continue beyond the checkpoint. That authorization was given only to government employees and private contractors who had passed an extensive background check, including at least one polygraph screening, and subsequently received additional training in the handling of materials with the designation SCI— Sensitive Compartmentalized Information. According to the information contained in the chip of the "smart" card, Ryan Duarte, a computer information specialist employed by Booz Allen Hamilton, had completed the requisite vetting process and was so authorized.

After about a minute, the card reader beeped and the guard removed the card and handed it back, along with a holographic facility-specific visitor's identification badge.

"Make sure this is visible at all times," the guard said.

Jimmy Letson thanked the guard and clipped the badge to his shirt front, before heading through to the waiting area for the on-campus shuttle. He waited until he was out of the guard's line of sight to let out the breath he had been holding.

"One down," he muttered. "Ninety-nine to go."

It was a joke, of course. While there were in fact well over a hundred security checkpoints on the campus, he would only have to go through about a dozen or so. He would be searched and questioned, required to leave all his possessions in a secure locker, and then searched and questioned some more.

The card, along with the Ryan Duarte persona, was something he had created years before with the help of a confidential source inside the NSA. He had used it from time to time in his investigations to discreetly confirm claims from other sources, but always remotely, spoofing the login with his own computer equipment. With his computer compromised, that was no longer an option, which meant it was time for his alter-ego to make his debut public appearance.

He wasn't worried about giving himself away. As a reporter, he'd bluffed his way into places with even tighter security. His real concern was that the Duarte alias might also be compromised. If that was the case, they wouldn't arrest him at the front gate; no, they'd wait until he did something really illegal.

Like using his bogus credentials to log into a computer terminal to access and delete server logs.

He still had no idea what was going on or who was stalking him. All he knew for certain was that, a few days earlier while conducting some seemingly innocuous research for his friend Dane Maddock someone had initiated a back-trace on him, systematically preventing him from erasing the logs of the proxy servers he routinely employed to mask his IP address. What was really unusual, not to mention alarming, was the speed with which the back-trace had been executed. There were few agencies in the world with the resources to do that. The NSA was definitely one of them.

Yet, he didn't think the American government was behind this action. For one thing, the servers he used as proxies were all in foreign countries—countries which did not cooperate with American law enforcement in the investigation of cyber-crimes. For another, he had not actually done anything illegal. And to the best of his knowledge, there was nothing sensitive about the research subject.

Maddock and his crew had discovered an old plane wreck off the coast of South Africa. The discovery of the plane—a Boeing 314 Clippership, manufactured in the 1930s—was unusual because only twelve such aircraft had ever been produced, and all twelve were accounted for. Jimmy had poked around in some historical archives and found nothing. Maddock had also recovered an artifact, a steel hatchet head engraved with a name and a presentation date—Steven Thorne. April 28, 1758—and apparently infused with some kind of metal that resisted corrosion. His research into that had similarly ended with no results. That should have been the end of the matter, but when he went to erase his digital footprints from the server logs, he discovered that he had already been frozen out.

Jimmy had gone to great lengths to safeguard himself, but there was no way to know for sure if those measures had worked. Panicking, he had severed the connection, shut his network down, and walked away.

Yet, he knew that running was no solution. It was not an exaggeration to say that computers were his life. He had spent more than two decades building his virtual existence, networking, mapping systems, finding backdoors and shortcuts. His pride and joy, NAILS—a heuristic deep-web search engine for prowling the deepest reaches of the dark net—represented an investment of thousands of hours and was, as far as he was concerned, completely irreplaceable. Starting over with a new identity simply wasn't an option. Which left him only one course of action: He had to get his life back.

At a minimum, that would involve erasing the evidence of his search for the plane crash and the hatchet. From the NSA, he would be able to override whatever security measures had been used to block his access to the server logs. With a little luck, he might also be able to identify the entity responsible for that action, which would be of paramount importance in determining his next course of action.

Once he was inside, he went to one of the workstations designated for use by visiting personnel, and began the login process. As nerve-wracking as the multiple redundant security checks had been, logging into the workstation was even worse. What if the NSA was the agency that had blocked him? What if they knew about the Duarte alias, and were waiting for him to commit himself? What if—

The seal of the National Security Agency—a bald eagle, standing behind a shield with the color-scheme of an American flag, gripping an old-fashioned skeleton key in its talons—appeared on the screen, along with a simple welcome message.

Jimmy blew out his breath, and immediately began navigating to the first of several IP addresses he had earlier used as proxies to spoof his location. He was pleased to see that the system administrator login information had not changed, which would have been the first thing a real sysadmin would do following an intrusion, but his relief was short-lived. When he brought up the logs for the relevant time period, he found that the information had already been deleted. He checked another IP address in the proxy chain with the same result. Someone had beaten him to the punch.

He dug deeper into the maintenance logs, trying to find the identity of the person or agency who had made those alterations, but that information also appeared to have been scrubbed clean.

A cold lump of disappointment began to form in Jimmy's gut. He checked the next proxy server in the chain, then another and yet another, but with the same result each time.

He checked the session timer. Almost ten minutes had elapsed since his login. In the age of high-speed data transfer, that was an eternity. Had the entity responsible for scrubbing the logs noticed him sniffing around? If so, it was already too late to do anything about it, but he felt an almost overwhelming urge to get moving. The longer he stayed, the greater his chances of being found out.

But as he was about to log out, inspiration struck. He went back to the logs, and one by one, examined each one, but this time, he opened the figurative window a little wider. He scrolled down the list of IP addresses for other users who had accessed the server within half an hour either way of his original search, and then did the same with each of the other servers looking for repeats.

It was a longshot, he knew, since any hacker worth his or her salt would almost certainly have spoofed a different IP address for each intrusion, but sometimes even the best made stupid little mistakes. Like re-using a spoofed server.

There it was.

The same IP address appeared on two different server logs.

It might have been a coincidence, but Jimmy felt certain it was not.

A trail of multiple proxies eventually led him to the SvalSat data hub in Norway and no further. Jimmy's gut told him it probably wasn't the original location of the hacker, but it was the end of the proxy chain.

And the end of what he could accomplish here.

He memorized the information and then, after doing what he could to cover his own tracks, logged off.

For a while after that, he just sat there, staring at the blank monitor, wondering what to do next. He was reasonably certain that no US government agency was responsible; they would not have erased the evidence of his intrusion….

Unless….

It occurred to him that he might have misread the situation completely. He had been working under the assumption that the entity in question was trying to track him down, either to arrest him or make him disappear, but what if they were simply trying to cover something up?

Instead of trying to figure out who's responsible, he thought, *I should be trying to figure out what's so important about that old plane wreck.*

But was it safe for him to go back home, return to his life—his computer—and carry on as if nothing had happened?

He pondered this a few seconds longer, and then realized that was the wrong question, too. Maybe it wasn't safe, but he was done running. He had skills, after all.

He took a deep breath, found his center and stood up from the workstation. Some part of him still half-expected a squad of agents to materialize and surround him, but nobody in the building seemed to pay him any special attention. The guards searched him perfunctorily to make sure he wasn't trying to leave with any classified data, and then returned his checked belongings to him and bade him good day. His fellow passengers on the shuttle back to the visitors' welcome center didn't even look his way, and when he handed back his temporary ID badge, the guard actually smiled at him.

As he started the rental car and pulled out of his parking spot, Jimmy shifted his mental gears to his next task. With the illicit foray into the nation's premier intelligence gathering service behind him, he would now return to where it had all started—the mysterious plane wreck. Maybe there wasn't a digital record, but there had to be a paper trail.

He steered out of the parking lot and onto Canine Road, following the signs to the onramp for the southbound lanes of the freeway.

He wondered if Maddock had discovered anything more about it, and made a mental note to contact the treasure hunter as soon—

The car abruptly jolted forward, and Jimmy's head snapped back a little, though not enough to cause any pain. The accompanying noise—like a car door slamming—left little doubt as to what had just occurred.

"What the hell?" he snarled, more irritated than angry. He glanced in the rearview mirror and saw the silver car that had just bumped him, still tailgating but backing away slowly.

A faint tingle of fear went through him. What if this was more than just a simple bumper-thumper? What if this was the enemy action he had been expecting all along?

The silver car's emergency flashers came on and then the vehicle pulled over into the breakdown lane and kept rolling forward slowly, subtly indicating that he should do the same. Jimmy slowed but did not pull over.

If this was just an ordinary traffic accident, he would need to stop, need to get the other driver's insurance information. He doubted there was any damage, but didn't want to be on the hook with the rental company for even minor repairs.

He looked around. There wasn't a lot of traffic on the road, but enough that if this was more than it seemed to be, he could start waving his arms frantically for help, or simply take off running. The NSA headquarters building was only about two hundred feet away, and he wouldn't have to even reach the building to get the attention of the security guards.

Unless of course they're the ones behind this, he thought. *But then why let me leave the building?* "You're just being paranoid, Jimmy," he muttered to himself.

He flipped on his turn signal and pulled to the side, but left the engine on, the automatic transmission still in gear, his foot on the brake. If this went sideways, or if he just got a funny feeling, all he would have to do is stomp on the gas pedal.

The silver car stopped a couple lengths behind him and the driver—a tall lanky man, dressed in jeans with a button-up work shirt and wearing a brown Indiana Jones-style fedora—got out and began advancing toward Jimmy's door. The brim of the hat mostly hid the man's face; other than his race—Caucasian—Jimmy couldn't determine much else about the man. He surreptitiously checked to make sure his door was locked and then cracked the window a few inches.

The man tipped his hat back, exposing a face that, while smiling, appeared taciturn. He looked to be about the same age as Jimmy, and there was something vaguely familiar about him, but Jimmy couldn't put his finger on it.

The man placed one hand on the roof of the car and leaned down, putting his face close to the gap in the window, and as he did, the smile slipped completely away. "Hello, Letson. Been a while, huh?"

3.

Professor felt the car start to move. He'd thought
he detected a hint of recognition when he'd
approached, but now Jimmy was freaking out.

"Letson, it's me. Pete Chapman. We did Phase
One together. I was in the teams. I served with Dane
and Bones."

The car lurched as Jimmy stomped down on the
brake again. "Professor?"

The nasally voice was like nails on a chalkboard,
transporting Professor back in time.

Can't do it. I quit.

Professor managed a nod. "That's me."

Jimmy's face registered a range of expressions.
Surprise, dismay… Embarrassment? Professor
could almost see the gears turning behind the other
man's eyes, and imagined him being sucked into the
same remembrance of their brief acquaintance.

But he wasn't interested in taking Jimmy for a
walk down memory lane. "Let's exchange our info,
just like this was a real accident."

"It felt pretty real to me," Jimmy remarked
sourly, then he cocked his head to the side. "Wait a
sec. You hit me on purpose. What's going on? What
do you want?" A pause, and then, "Who are you
working for?"

Professor ignored the question. "Letson, you
need to tell me what you were doing in there.

Whatever it is, whatever laws you've broken, I can't help you if you don't tell me the truth."

"What makes you think I want your help?" Jimmy shot back.

Professor sighed.

"You're working for Tam Broderick's outfit, aren't you?" Jimmy pressed. "Yeah, I know all about that. Dane told me some of it, and I figured out the rest."

"That's great, Letson. So, you know I'm one of the good guys. My question is, are you?"

"Oh, so working for the government automatically equals good guys. I'll have to remember that."

"Knock it off, Letson," Professor snapped. "You just walked out of a Secure Compartmented Information Facility, and we both know that you don't have a security clearance, which tells me that, at the very least, you presented falsified credentials. That's a crime. Fortunately for you, I'm not a cop or I'd have to arrest you right now. But you've got about thirty seconds to convince me that *you* are one of the good guys, before I *do* call the cops, so don't waste it… Twenty-nine… Twenty-eight…"

Jimmy glowered for about three more seconds, then looked down just long enough to move the gearshift lever into park, and roll the window the rest of the way down. That gave him about twenty seconds, but Professor figured the point was made, so he stopped counting. As Jimmy launched into an explanation of the events that had prompted him to go off the grid, Professor raised a hand to stop him.

"Give me the Cliff's Notes version." What he really wanted was to confirm that Jimmy wasn't knowingly or unknowingly carrying out state-sponsored espionage.

"Maddock asked me to research an old plane wreck," Jimmy said. "When I tried, somebody came after me. I have no idea who or why, but they're good."

Professor blew out his cheeks. He wanted more details, but there was a time and place and this wasn't either. "All right, Dane trusts you. So does Tam in a weird grudging sort of way—"

Jimmy snorted with derisive laughter. "I'll have to add that to my CV."

"We can finish this conversation somewhere else," Professor went on. "But before we move an inch, I need your word that you aren't trying to remove classified materials from this site. We don't need the NSA coming after us."

"Trust me," Jimmy replied. "I know better than to…"

He trailed off as a car—a silver Ford Taurus—rushed past in the outside lane. Most of the vehicles that had gone by during their brief encounter had observed the courtesy of changing lanes to give them a wide berth, but the Ford passed close enough that Professor had to lean in to avoid being struck. As soon as the vehicle cleared the front end of Jimmy's rental, the driver cut to the right and slammed on the brakes, screeching to a stop diagonally in front of Jimmy's car.

"Crap!" Professor snarled. From the corner of his eye, he saw another car—same make but white—swerve off the road behind them, pulling in close behind his rental, blocking them in. There were two men in the car to the front, and probably at least as many in the car behind. He didn't need to know anything more than that to know that he and Jimmy were in serious trouble.

He reached for the door handle, already mentally choreographing how he would shove Jimmy into the passenger seat, take his place behind the wheel, bump his way out of the trap—

The door handle didn't move.

He pounded his fist on the roof. "Letson, open the—"

The doors of the blocking vehicles were thrown open in unison, the occupants emerging. The men seemed to have been turned out of the same mold—big, muscular frames covered in loose-fitting jackets; short, utilitarian haircuts. They were heavies. Mercs. Hired guns. Probably former military though probably not SEALs or Special Forces—operators knew the importance of blending in. These men weren't displaying weapons, but their strong-side hands were conspicuously under their jacket flaps, clearly signaling both possession and intent.

There was no time to explain himself to Jimmy, so instead Professor reached in through the open window, stabbing his finger down on the electronic lock button. All four doors unlocked with a mechanical click, but instead of opening the driver's door, Professor side-stepped to the rear-left passenger door, opened it, and climbed in.

"Punch it!"

Jimmy craned his head around, staring at Professor in disbelief. "What—?"

Outside, the four men were just moments away from reaching the car, at which point, if he and Jimmy were lucky, they would only be ordered out at gunpoint.

"Go! Drive!"

"We're blocked in."

"So?"

Jimmy's head snapped around to face front and without further questions, he put the still-idling car in gear. There was a grinding sound as he cranked the wheel, and then the car lurched into motion. The front end of the rented Hyundai swung to the left, forcing one of the heavies to dance out of the way, and then came to a jarring stop as it crunched into the rear end of the blocking vehicle.

Jimmy shifted into reverse, cranked the wheel the opposite way, and stomped the gas again. With a jolt, the Hyundai shot backward, its rear tires rolling off the pavement, bumping onto the soft gravel beyond. Just as quickly, Jimmy switched directions and the red sedan jumped back up onto the pavement and shot past the car and onto the roadway.

Professor kept watch on the four heavies and wasn't at all surprised to see them drawing their weapons.

"Head down!" he warned.

But the men did not fire, or if they did, the weapons were fitted with suppressors and none of the shots found their mark. Jimmy accelerated, drove under the overpass and into the turn that would bring them around in a rising circle to join the southbound freeway.

Professor risked a quick peek out the rear window and saw that the four men were returning to their vehicles, no doubt planning to give chase.

And probably calling in reinforcements, he thought. He brought his gaze forward just as the curve in the road eclipsed his view of the men.

"Any idea who those guys are?" he asked.

"I was going to ask you," Jimmy replied. "I don't think they were NSA."

Professor shook his head. "No. Definitely private sector."

Jimmy offered no comment, appearing instead to focus on the approach to the freeway. He maintained acceleration, merging into the light traffic. Professor didn't need to look back to know that the other two cars would soon close with them. Getting on the freeway had probably been a bad move, though realistically, there weren't a whole lot of other places they could have gone.

He shifted forward, leaning into the gap

between the front seats to get a better look at the road ahead. Jimmy was now moving with the flow of traffic—the speedometer showed them doing about seventy even though the posted speed limit was fifty-five miles per hour.

"Floor it," Professor advised. "We need to put some space between us and them. And we need to get onto surface streets, find somewhere to ditch this car."

"What if we get pulled over?"

"I doubt we will, but even if that happens, those guys won't try anything with a state trooper standing here."

Jimmy cocked his head to the side in a shrug of resignation and then pressed down on the accelerator, adding another five miles per hour to their speed, and as soon as he was clear, swung the car into the faster moving inside lane. A green sign over the left lane announced the next exit—Exit 9— NSA Employees Only.

"Crap again," Professor muttered. It would be at least another mile before they would get another opportunity to leave the freeway and hopefully ditch their pursuers, but going back to the National Security Agency headquarters wasn't an option. "Keep going. Take the next exit."

Jimmy nodded and continued weaving in and out of traffic, accelerating the whole time. The speedometer ticked up to eighty. Eighty-five. Yet Jimmy seemed cool as a cucumber.

"Pretty fancy driving there, Letson," Professor

admitted, grudgingly.

"It's just Jimmy. And thanks. I play a lot of GTA."

"GTA?"

"Grand Theft Auto. PlayStation. You know, video games?"

"Ah," Professor said, now a little less impressed. "Well maybe dial it down a little. There's no reset button for this game."

"Reset button." Jimmy snorted, wagging his head. "Okay, Dad, whatever you say."

"Dad? We're the same age."

"Could've fooled me."

"This isn't a game, Letson. Whatever you were running from just caught up with you. And I just happen to have a bit more experience dealing with the real world life and death stuff."

"Is that a fact? You know, I was doing just fine before you decided to rear-end me, so maybe you're not the best person to be giving me advice about the real world."

Professor shuffled through his deck of scathing retorts but decided he had better things to do. "Take the next exit, whatever it is."

"Exit eight," Jimmy said, answering the unasked question. "Fort Mead and Laurel."

"You know the area?"

"Pretty well. There's an airport just off the exit."

"Airport?" Professor sat up a little straighter.

"A small one. Three-thousand-foot runway. Mostly services single-engine planes. A few helicopters."

The seed of a plan began to take root in Professor's mind. "Perfect. Go there."

"Awesome," Jimmy said, with more than a hint of sarcasm. "Are we going to charter a plane, or just steal one?"

"I don't know. Did Grand Theft Auto teach you how to fly, too?"

"Actually, yeah. Though I prefer Flight Simulator. More realistic."

Professor shook his head wearily. "Just get us to the airport. I'll take care of the rest."

A few seconds later, another sign heralded Tipton Airport, and Professor spotted the exit lane veering off to the right. Jimmy waited until the last second to cut across both lanes and steered onto the upward sloping ramp, slowing a little as he neared the crest and entered the traffic circle at the top. As he did, Professor looked back again and saw several cars coming up the ramp behind them; he recognized two of them—the silver and white Ford sedans that had tried to block them earlier.

"Damn it," he muttered. His plan had been to ditch the car at the airport and then hoof it into the woods, hoping the men chasing them would assume they had boarded a plane, but to make it convincing, they would need a little more lead time. "Okay, forget the airport for now. Blow past and just try to lose these guys."

Jimmy feathered the brakes as he went into the soft right at the traffic circle, curling back around, but halfway through the turn, he began accelerating again. The tires squealed a little as G-forces pulled them to the left, but Jimmy deftly steered out of the slide and maintained pressure on the gas pedal as they shot down the country road.

The turn-off to the airport flashed by, and then the road narrowed to an ordinary two-lane country road. Off to the right, on the far side of a wetland, Professor could see the freeway running parallel to their current course, but then the road curved to the left leaving both the marsh and the freeway behind.

Though he was loath to admit it, Professor thought Jimmy was handling the situation pretty well. Maybe video games were good for something more than just mindless entertainment. But as capable as he seemed, Jimmy's virtual driving practice was no match for the kind of tactical driving instruction Professor had received in the SEALs, and judging by the quickness with which they were closing the gap, the men in the chase cars had taken the same course.

The silver car rocketed down the straightaway and was just a hundred yards—and maybe five seconds—behind them as they entered the turn. Professor could make out the hard visages of the two heavies in the front seats. They weren't showing guns which meant they were probably going to try to force the Hyundai off the road.

Probably.

"Letson—"

"Jimmy!"

"Fine, Jimmy. Do exactly as I tell you, when I tell you. No questions. Got it?"

He expected questions, but Jimmy just said, "Yeah."

Behind them, the lead car abruptly swung into the left lane and shot forward again—the driver had to be pushing over the century mark—and blew past them like they were standing still. Professor tracked them for a second, then glanced back and saw the second Ford closing from the rear.

"They're trying to box us in," he said.

Right on cue, the silver Ford pulled back into the right lane a hundred yards or more ahead of them, brake lights flaring red as the driver started shedding speed. Jimmy reflexively tapped his brakes, too, even though the other car was still several lengths ahead.

"No," Professor shouted. "Floor it."

"But—" Jimmy started to say, but then cut himself off and did as instructed, depressing the accelerator. The Hyundai shot forward, rapidly closing with the lead car, which was still slowing. The driver of the silver Ford, still following the playbook, turned diagonally, cutting the road and coming to a full stop right on top of the center line, blocking both lanes.

"Go left," Professor urged. "Pass him on the shoulder."

"Left? But what if—" Jimmy caught himself again, and after waiting a beat, cranked the wheel over, aiming for the shoulder on the far side of the road.

Professor knew why Jimmy had almost balked. The Taurus was blocking their view of the oncoming lane, and if anyone was trying to pass the Ford on the shoulder, the Hyundai would hit them head-on. But it was the last thing the men in the Ford would expect them to do, and therefore was exactly what had to be done. Hopefully, the shoulder would be clear.

It wasn't.

A pickup, still partially shrouded behind a cloud of rubber smoke after slamming on its brakes to avoid hitting the Ford, was just beginning to pull onto the shoulder in order to pass. Jimmy, to his credit, did not put on the brakes, but pushed the throttle harder, whipping the Hyundai hard to the right, threading the gap between the front end of the pickup and the silver car.

He almost made it.

The right front corner of the Taurus caught the Hyundai's right side with an ugly crunching sound. The impact pushed the Ford sideways, which caused the left corner to swing into the Hyundai's flanks but then with a torturous squeal, Jimmy's car broke free and rocketed ahead as he stomped the gas pedal to the floor.

"Yeah," he chortled. "That's what I'm talking about."

"Better than video games, right?" Professor said, unable to hide a grin.

"Yeah. Except I'll be on the hook for the

damage."

"Should have signed the waiver," Professor replied, still grinning. He checked behind them and saw the Ford just starting to move again, then returned his gaze to the road ahead. They were approaching some commercial buildings. A gas station and a general store on the right, a restaurant or tavern on the left. He almost told Jimmy to pull off and park the car, lie low and hope their pursuers would pass them by, but the trailing cars were still within easy visual range, and the parking lots were small and sparsely occupied.

He looked further down the road to where the trees returned and spotted a sign and a turn lane that seemed to plunge straight into the woods. "Think you can make that right turn up there?"

Jimmy leaned forward a little as if to get a better look. "You mean without slowing down? I can try."

"Do it."

The Hyundai surged a little as Jimmy revved the gas, but then he eased up, letting the car coast the rest of the way to the exit. "Hang on!" he shouted, though the warning wasn't necessary, and then hauled the wheel sharply to the right. The tires screeched on the pavement. Professor could feel the right side of the vehicle growing lighter, trying to take off—or flip over—but gravity won out. The car skidded into the turn and Jimmy accelerated again, and just like that they were shooting down the narrow tree-lined lane. The road curved a little to the left, then continued straight for a couple hundred yards before turning left again.

Perfect, Professor thought, and then added aloud, "Get around that bend as soon as you can, then find a place to pull off. Left side would be best, but just get us into the woods."

He kept watch out the rear window while Jimmy raced the Hyundai to the turn. The road behind them remained empty, at least until the turn blocked his view of it. He craned his head forward again, scanning the road ahead until he saw what he was looking for. "There," he shouted, stabbing a finger over Jimmy's shoulder. "Hard left."

Jimmy cranked the wheel and the Hyundai squealed across the road and into a paved turnout— a parking area for the welcome center on the opposite side of the road.

"Turn it around," Professor said. "And back into the woods. Hurry."

Jimmy complied without comment, executing a surprisingly close approximation of a bootlegger's turn—surprising since the rental had an automatic transmission, front-wheel drive and anti-lock brakes. The Hyundai whipped around one-hundred-and-eighty degrees to face the road. There was a slight jolt as the rear wheels skidded off the edge of the pavement and onto the soft grassy earth beyond, and then another as Jimmy powered forward, bringing the car up close to the woods at the edge of the parking area.

"Head down," Professor instructed. "But be

ready to take off."

"I got it," Jimmy said, a little irritably. "We're going to fake them out and then head back the other way. I'm not as stupid as you seem to think."

Professor frowned but let the comment pass. He hunched over, staying low behind Jimmy's seat, watching the road.

The wait was interminable. "Think we lost them?" Jimmy asked.

"Not yet." It felt like they had been waiting for several minutes, but Professor had been watching the sweep second hand of his Omega wristwatch and knew that just thirty seconds had passed.

Fifteen more seconds ticked by and then without any warning whatsoever, the silver Taurus burst from behind the trees, racing past. The white Ford was only a few car lengths behind. Neither one slowed, the drivers evidently hyper-focused on the road and catching up to their elusive prey.

"Wait for it," Professor warned.

The two vehicles continued down the road, passing out of view.

"Now. Get us back to the road."

Jimmy had the car moving before the command was finished. He steered back onto the road and accelerated away. Professor kept a constant vigil to their rear, watching for any sign that the pursuers had grown wise to the deception. It occurred to him that they, like himself, might have tagged Jimmy's car, but that seemed unlikely. If the heavies had been tracking Jimmy all along, they wouldn't have made their move when and where they had, nor would they have waited until he was done at the NSA. The more plausible explanation was that they had come in response to something Jimmy had done—another silent alarm triggered by his investigation.

Jimmy had definitely kicked a hornet's nest.

The road behind them stayed clear all the way to the bend leading back to the road, and for the first time since the chase began, Professor allowed himself a small sigh of relief.

"Where to?" Jimmy asked as they rounded the last bend, slowing to pull back onto the main road. "Should I go back to the airport?"

"Let's head back to the freeway," Professor turned around. "I'll take you to a safe house—Look out!"

It came from out of nowhere, an ominous black shape—an SUV or pickup—rushing at them from their right. There was no time to react, barely time to brace for the collision.

Not that it did any good.

4.

Professor awoke with a start, and for a few sublime seconds, felt nothing more than mild confusion at the unfamiliarity of his surroundings.

Then the pain arrived like a cartoon anvil dropping from the sky on his head.

The total-body muscle pain triggered a memory—the black truck coming from out of nowhere to T-bone Jimmy's rental car.

"Jimmy!" he said, almost shouting.

To his utter astonishment, he heard the other man's voice. "Hey, he's awake!"

Professor sat up, gritting his teeth against the pain. He felt woozy, and for a moment wondered if he had sustained a concussion, but dismissed that explanation; this felt more like a narcotic fog.

Another memory percolated up. He was back in the car, covered in broken glass and partially pinned by a collapsed segment of the frame… A man in a blue uniform—a paramedic?—leaning over him, urging him to remain calm, promising that they would have him out in a few seconds… And then the man had reached in with a hypodermic syringe, a drop of fluid glistening at the needle's tip.

This will help calm you down.

He looked around, his brain finally processing the visual stimuli. He wasn't in a hospital, nor was he in anything that resembled a prison cell. Rather, he appeared to be in a library, or perhaps a private museum. Three walls of the elegantly appointed room were lined with floor to ceiling bookshelves, but only about half of the shelves sported leather and cloth bound books. The rest held an eclectic display of artifacts—souvenirs from cultures around the globe and across history, along with several pieces of nautical memorabilia. It was the kind of place, Professor thought, where Dane Maddock would feel right at home.

The hardwood floor was covered by a beautiful Persian carpet. The remaining wall was mostly windows and a set of French doors with glass panels that looked out over a somber landscape of trees denuded with the onset of winter.

"Toto, I've a feeling we're not in Maryland anymore," he muttered, struggling to sit up.

"You got that right," Jimmy said, stepping into view.

Professor blinked to bring the other man into focus. Jimmy had changed clothes. There was an abrasion on his left cheek, but he appeared otherwise uninjured. He definitely didn't look like a prisoner or a hostage.

"Where are we?"

"New York," intoned another voice—masculine and booming, but friendly enough. "Long Island to be precise. Welcome to my home… Professor is it?"

Long Island? That meant he'd been unconscious for several hours.

Professor turned slowly, not trusting that his equilibrium was fully restored, and located Jimmy and the other man. The latter—their host—was about the same height as Jimmy, but considerably older, early seventies, Professor guessed, with tousled hair that was more salt than pepper and a full beard that was all white. His skin was deeply tanned, his high forehead creased with a map of wrinkles, but his blue eyes were clear and twinkled like sapphires. He was smiling, and his body language showed no hint of aggression, nor did Jimmy seem the least bit on his guard in the man's presence, but Professor remained wary.

"My friends call me that," he said.

The man laughed. "Fair enough, Dr. Chapman. My name is Christian Garral. You may call me Christian. As you like."

"Garral? You're Nick Kismet's father." Professor immediately regretted blurting the revelation.

The man's bushy white eyebrows arched in surprise. "You know my son?"

He had recognized the name from his earlier reading of the files of the man who had helped Jade and he out of a sticky situation in Peru. Nick Kismet worked for the Global Heritage Commission—a United Nations agency tasked with monitoring World Heritage sites and protecting international antiquities. Kismet had actually been in South America looking for them, or rather for Jade, on personal business. He was seeking information about a manuscript that had belonged to famed

British occultist Dr. John Dee, and thought Jade, who had dealt with a notorious collector of Dee memorabilia a couple years earlier, might have some special insight on the matter. Kismet's arrival had been both serendipitous and suspicious, but a cursory check of his bona fides had impressed Tam Broderick enough to recommend that Jade stay with Kismet and help him out while Professor looked into the matter of Jimmy's disappearance.

But now the trail had circled back to a connection with Nick Kismet. Professor didn't believe in coincidences, and this was a hell of a big one.

And he had just tipped his hand.

Nothing to do about it now, he thought. *Might as well call.*

"Evidently, not very well," he replied. "I bumped into him in South America a couple days ago. He was looking for information and thought my partner Jade Ihara could help him."

Garral nodded. "Ah, yes. The *Liber Arcanum.* My boy does get around."

Professor searched the craggy face for any sign of duplicity, but saw none at all. Garral clapped his hands together. "I'm sorry, you must be full of questions about what has happened. But first, how are you feeling? Do you require additional medical attention?"

"I was drugged," Professor accused. "Was that your doing?"

"It was. My men didn't know who you were or what your intentions were, respecting Mr. Letson here." He paused and then corrected. "Jimmy, rather."

It was a small detail, but telling. Jimmy's insistence on the use of the familiar indicated that he had been won over by their host.

"My intentions were to keep him out of trouble."

"Yes, he explained it to us. We didn't realize—"

"Who's we?" Professor snapped.

For the first time since entering the room, Garral appeared discomfited, but what Professor first took for irritation was soon revealed as something else altogether.

"Go on," Jimmy urged. "Tell him what you told me."

"This will sound a bit like the stuff of conspiracy theories, but Jimmy assures me you have some experience with such things." Garral took a deep breath, let it out with a sigh. "There is a very powerful, and very old, organization—a secret society, if you like—that is secretly manipulating the destiny of humankind."

"The Dominion."

Garral shook his head. "No. At least, I don't believe they are one and the same, though in the shadowy world where these groups operate, it is difficult to say. They call themselves Prometheus, named for the Titan of Greek mythology."

Professor nodded. "Prometheus was especially

fond of humans. He stole fire from the gods and gave it to men. And he put hope in Pandora's box."

"You are correct. Prometheus is often associated with the gift of foresight. A thoughtful figure who anticipates trouble and takes pre-emptive action, unlike his brother Epimetheus."

"Prometheus is also the name of a high IQ society which restricts membership to those who score in the ninety-ninth percentile. I don't suppose that's who you're talking about."

Garral chuckled. "That group takes its name and inspiration from the group of which I speak, but to the best of my knowledge, there is no direct relationship. The real Prometheus organization has roots that go much deeper. It has existed in many forms, going back perhaps as far as the Athenians in the Greek classical period, but its current incarnation began during the Enlightenment. As men began expanding their knowledge of the cosmos…" He paused a beat. "Pardon me. That is a Western conceit. I should say, as Europeans began broadening their horizons, moving forward toward the Renaissance, there were some who believed that humans were on the verge of opening up another sort of Pandora's box. A trap, left behind, perhaps unintentionally, by an ancient forgotten race of beings."

Professor ignored the obvious question, focusing instead on something else. "What do you mean by 'unintentionally'?"

"Imagine that this knowledge is a box of

matches, left on a shelf. Fire is what sets us apart from other animals. It is what made civilization possible, and yet in the hands of a child, it can be very dangerous. The knowledge and power of this ancient race is beyond even our current comprehension of the universe. We are children, and this is a kind of fire we're not ready for." He paused. "That's what Prometheus believes, at any rate.

"The knowledge is hidden—encoded, if you will—in the lore and traditions of all the world's religions. Tales of gods and fallen angels who walked among humans, even interbred with them. Stories of powerful devices—technology mistaken for magic. I'm sure you're familiar with many of the myths. The men of Prometheus have, for many centuries, dedicated themselves to finding these devices and hiding them away so that humanity will not be tempted toward self-annihilation. Prometheus invites only the best and brightest into its ranks. Intelligence and vision are essential, but candidates must also exhibit the wisdom and forethought of Prometheus himself. The location of their vault is a secret known only to the innermost circle."

Professor raised a hand. "You keep saying *they*. '*They* call themselves "Prometheus."' You're not part of it?"

Garral looked chagrined. "Not exactly, but that's a long story and a detour which will take me even further from answering your original question.

"The short explanation is that there is currently a power struggle for control of Prometheus. One faction—the radicals, for want of a better name—believes it is their destiny to use the knowledge and power which they have accumulated to take control of humanity's destiny. The other side favors the original mission. They are the traditionalists. Whichever side prevails will have control of their vast trove of knowledge and ancient technology." He hesitated, scrutinizing Professor for a moment, then went on. "My son—my adopted son—is very important to Prometheus. Particularly to the traditionalists. I'm not at liberty to go into detail about that, but suffice it to say, I was brought into their confidence."

"Okay," Professor said, nodding. He wasn't sure he believed the story about Prometheus, but he was satisfied that Garral believed it. "Let me see if I've got this right. Prometheus is in the business of tracking down and hiding artifacts purported to have supernatural power."

"Like Warehouse 13," Jimmy put in.

Professor frowned, but only partly because of the interruption. He had no idea what that reference meant, which surprised him. Probably something from a video game. He pushed ahead. "And something about that old plane wreck that Dane Maddock discovered was a loose thread that might have led back to Prometheus and their treasure trove. When Jimmy went poking around looking into it, it tripped an alarm and Prometheus went after him."

"That's mostly accurate," Garral said. "That plane and its occupants discovered an important site in Antarctica. They weren't a part of Prometheus, but when the organization learned of it, they took steps to erase the incident from the public record."

"And they're still trying to cover it up today. That's why they went after Jimmy."

"No," Garral said slowly. "It's a bit more complicated than that. You see, the radicals are weak. They're outsiders, and without direct access to the collection of artifacts, their only hope for victory is to find something new. Something that isn't in the collection yet."

"Like something from that site at Antarctica," Professor said.

Garral nodded. "There is something there—an ancient power source. Prometheus calls it 'the anomaly.' They've known of its existence for decades, but did not have its exact location, despite numerous expeditions to find it. So they placed trigger-alerts on search topics related to the original discovery."

"That old plane was at the top of the list," Jimmy added.

"And then waited for someone else to do the heavy lifting," Professor finished.

"The radicals desperately need to find the anomaly."

"And that's why they came after Jimmy?"

Garral shook his head. "No. I'm afraid nobody 'came after' him, at least nobody I'm aware of. The men you encountered were working for me, keeping an eye on Jimmy. My... Ah, contact inside Prometheus—one of the traditionalists—warned me that they might. When you accosted Jimmy outside the National Security Agency headquarters, they thought you might be working for the radicals, and intervened. I apologize for the misunderstanding."

"You could have made contact with Jimmy any time. Brought him up to speed. You didn't. You were dangling him out there as bait."

Garral spread his hands in an apologetic gesture. "A mistake on my part," he admitted. "I realize that now. I should have brought Jimmy into my confidence. But you'll be safe here, provided you stay below the radar."

"What about Dane Maddock?" Professor asked. "The radicals might go after him as well."

"Way ahead of you, dude... er... Professor. I tried to call him first thing. Believe it or not, he's already looking for the anomaly doohickey. Although, I'm not sure he knows it. I talked to Willis."

Willis was Willis Sanders, another former SEAL swim buddy, currently crewing on Dane Maddock's boat, *Sea Foam*.

"Maddock and Bones headed for Antarctica a few hours ago. They're pretty much incommunicado down there."

"So there's no way to warn them." Professor glanced at Garral. "I don't suppose you've got the resources to get us down there."

Jimmy threw his hands up in protest. "Whoa, what's with this 'us' stuff? And in case you've forgotten, Antarctica is a big place. We don't even know where to start looking."

"Maddock had to have left a paper trail. You can track that down. And I can have Tam task a satellite in polar orbit to look for him."

Garral spread his hands helplessly. "Time is the resource in shortest supply. There aren't exactly direct flights into Antarctica. It would take several days just to get you to an airport with service to the continent. By then, it may be too late."

Professor pondered this for a moment. Garral was right. It had taken him nearly two days just to travel from Peru to Maryland.

He broke into a grin as an idea dawned. "There are flights from Argentina to Antarctica, right? If we had somebody already on the ground in South America, that would cut a couple days off our response time."

Garral nodded, thoughtfully. "You're referring to your friend Jade Ihara?"

"And your son."

"They may have already left."

Professor shrugged. "Can't hurt to ask."

Jimmy let out a low whistle. "You want to send Jade off to rescue Maddock. I can't imagine how that might go horribly wrong."

PART TWO: WISDOM OF THE AGES

5.

"I knew this would go horribly wrong," Uriah "Bones" Bonebrake muttered, shaking his head in disgust.

"Silence," hissed the young blond-haired man who held a pistol pressed to the side of Jade Ihara's neck.

"What do you want, Black?" Dane Maddock asked.

"You know what I want," sneered Aramis Black. "Give them to me now, or she dies."

Aramis Black—that was the name the man had given them a few days earlier when they had first met but probably not the name on his birth certificate—was a magician. Not a sleight-of-hand illusionist, but an honest to goodness sorcerer, a student of the dark arts which, Maddock thought, might explain how he had been able to sneak up on them, seemingly materializing out of thin air, to grab Jade and put a gun to her throat.

Black belonged to an occult society based in Plymouth, England, presently led by an exotic raven-haired beauty named Aliyah Cerulean. Aliyah and Black, along with the other members of their order, had until recently been the guardians of a purportedly magical talisman which they called "the Magna of Illusion," an obsidian mirror found in a temple ruin in Central America in the Sixteenth Century and allegedly owned by famed occultist Dr. John Dee, who had used it for divination and prophecy.

Maddock had no idea if any of that was true, but the mirror was real enough. He knew this for a fact because he—along with Jade and Bones, and their new companions, Rose Greer and Nick Kismet— had stolen the Magna of Illusion from the order's treasure vault on Drake Island in Plymouth Harbor.

Maybe "stolen" wasn't the right word.

Aliyah, had drawn them into a trap so that she could seize two relics which were in their possession: The Apex, an amulet of blue stone in the shape of a pyramid, discovered more than a century earlier by an ancestor of Kismet's adopted father; and a black metallic sphere, which they had dubbed "the orb" but which Kismet sometimes called "the anomaly," discovered in an ice-bound pyramid in Antarctica just a week before.

The three objects—the Apex, the orb and the mirror—were part of a set, it seemed; three of four, each representing a different alchemical element— fire, earth, water, and air—and each linked to a suit in the mystical Tarot deck—wands, disks, cups, and swords. The search for the fourth relic was what had brought Maddock and his friends to the ruins of ancient Tyana, on the Anatolian Plateau of central Turkey.

Aliyah desired all four relics, believing that they would imbue her with immortality and other supernatural gifts. She had also expressed a desire to kill Nick Kismet, in revenge for the death of her husband, who had perished while attempting to steal the Apex from Kismet. The five of them had turned the tables on Aliyah and her magicians, escaping with all three artifacts, which seemed to Maddock like fair restitution for the trouble she had put them through. Evidently, Aliyah Cerulean had a different definition of "fair."

Bones shrugged in response to the threat. "Kill her. It's no skin off my handsomely aquiline Cherokee nose."

Jade glowered at him. "Maybe we should trade places, *Uriah*."

"She will only be the first to die," Black hissed, shaking her for effect. "And lest you think you can repeat that little trick you used against us on Drake's Island, know that there are sniper rifles trained on you at this very moment."

"'Lest'?" Bones said, giving Maddock a sidelong glance. "Who talks like that?"

Maddock ignored his friend. The quips were just Bones' way of dealing with stressful situations. And pretty much every other kind of situation, too.

"How did you find us?" he asked.

His curiosity was genuine, since they had taken great pains to disguise their movements from England to Turkey, but he didn't really need an answer to the question. What he was really doing was stalling. The sniper threat felt like a bluff. On the flat plain where the ruins were situated, there weren't a lot of places with a good line of sight, though there was a stand of trees to the northwest where, conceivably, a gunman might be able to reach sufficient elevation to draw a bead on them. Maddock wasn't ready to call that bluff just yet.

Another familiar voice spoke from behind them, answering the question. "You seek the Tabula Smaragdina," said Aliyah Cerulean. "Where else would you go?"

The Tabula Smaragdina—the Emerald Tablet—was an alchemical, or more accurately, hermetical text which purported to contain the secret for creating *prima materia*—the key ingredient in the so-called Philosopher's Stone—which could be used to create an elixir of eternal life or transmute base metals into gold.

The text was well known, handed down through the centuries, translated and studied by great thinkers such as Roger Bacon, Albert Magnus, Sir Isaac Newton and even Carl Jung. The text included one of the key principles of alchemy, "As above, so below," but also hinted at a relationship between matter and energy which would not be understood until the dawn of the nuclear age. The origin of the short text—just fourteen lines—was uncertain, but the oldest documentable source of the text was found in an Eighth Century Persian manuscript called *Kitāb sirr al-ḥalīqa*—the Book of the Secret of Creation and the Art of Nature—attributed to a man named Balinas. Balinas, also called Pseudo-Apollonius of Tyana—claimed to have copied it from a tablet made of emerald—thus the name—which he had discovered in a vault below a statue of Hermes in the city of Tyana.

Maddock would have dismissed the story as fanciful if not for the fact that Nick Kismet had seen something that looked remarkably like an emerald tablet in a vision supplied by the Magna of Illusion. There seemed little doubt that the Emerald Tablet—not the text, but the original tablet itself—was the fourth elemental relic.

Maddock turned his head in the direction of the voice and saw Aliyah, flanked by two men with guns, presumably other members of her occult order.

"You obviously already have the sphere from the ice pyramid," Aliyah went on. "That's the only explanation for the power you used to defeat us at Plymouth. Only the sword remains—the elemental talisman representing air. The Smaragdine Tablet."

Maddock shrugged. "The legend says that Balinas found the Emerald Tablet in a vault under the statue of Hermes in Tyana. It seemed like the place to start looking."

Aliyah gave a cold laugh. "And it did not occur

to you that others would have searched this place before you?" She shook her head. "Your ignorance amply demonstrates that you are not worthy to possess the elemental talismans."

"What's that supposed to mean?" asked Bones.

Aliyah waved a hand. "There is no statue of Hermes here. No temple."

That was something Maddock and the others had learned even before boarding the flight to Ankara, Turkey. The ruins of Tyana consisted mainly of some arches supporting a Roman aqueduct and a public bath. The rest of the city, which had once been an important settlement in the region going back to the time of the Hittite Empire in the Second Millennium B.C.E., was gone—buried under the sands of time.

"Maybe not anymore," Maddock conceded.

Aliyah laughed again. "And you imagined that, if you could find the place where it once stood, the vault would magically open to you, as it did for Balinas."

"Stranger things have happened," Maddock said, shrugging.

In truth, that was exactly what they had been hoping for. The four elemental relics were linked somehow, reacting visibly when in close proximity with each other, and they had hoped to use the three relics they possessed like a compass to lead them to the fourth.

"Is it really so hard to believe?" Bones added. "Come on. I thought you guys believed in magic."

He drew out the last consonant and then added, "With a 'k'."

Magick, as they had learned, was the preferred spelling for the occultists, a way of differentiating their 'serious' magical practices from the trickery of stage magicians.

"Give me the elemental talismans," Aliyah said, her tone as cold and hard as a glacier, "and I will let you walk away."

"Joke's on you," Bones said. "We don't have them. Kismet and Rose took them. They didn't tell us where."

"Somewhere where they'll be safe from you," Maddock confirmed with a nod. "You didn't really think we'd just wander around with them in a backpack, did you?"

Aliyah's eyes narrowed, as if focusing laser beams of pure hate energy at them. "Then there's no reason to bother with you any longer, is there?"

"Right?" Bones said. "See ya."

Aliyah turned to one of the men beside her. "Kill them."

Maddock sucked in his breath. "Are you sure you want to do that? Out here in the open?"

Aliyah's lips curled into a malevolent smile. "Do you see anyone else here?"

"Let me guess. You bribed the local police to keep everyone away so there wouldn't be any witnesses."

Aliyah inclined her head. "Like I said, I knew you would come here." She looked away and made a cutting gesture, signaling her desire to end the conversation. Permanently.

"Wait," Bones said, quickly. "I lied."

"What a surprise." Aliyah did not look at him, but the two gunmen with her did. They raised their pistols and took aim.

Bones pressed on. "When I said I didn't know where Kismet was going to take those magical doohickeys… That was a fib. I do know."

Aliyah shrugged. "I think this is the lie. But it does not matter. I found you. I will find him."

The gunmen circled around behind Maddock and Bones, maintaining a stand-off distance of several feet. "Kneel," one of them said. "Hands behind your head. Fingers laced."

"You saw that in a movie, right?" Bones retorted. "Trust me, it's a whole lot different in real life." He didn't sound even a little bit fearful, which was more than Maddock could say for himself.

Where is Kismet, he wondered.

A foot struck him in the back of the knee and his leg folded under him, dropping him into a kneeling position.

"Wait!" cried out a new voice. A woman's voice.

Maddock looked up and saw Rose Greer approaching, her hands raised. The straps of her backpack were visible, crossing over the top of her shoulders, looping around her arms. Maddock's heart sank a little lower. The backpack contained two of the relics—the orb and the mirror.

Aliyah faced Rose. "Ah, what a surprise. Now we're just missing one. Where is Nick Kismet?"

"He's out there. Watching." Rose kept her head high, defiant, but there was still a faint quaver of fear in her voice. She locked stares with Maddock. "He told me to tell you that he took care of the sniper. He also said you should look for the laser dot."

The effect of these words on Aliyah's magicians was immediate and dramatic. The men began looking around, checking themselves to see if they were being painted with the red dot of a laser aiming device, and as they did, their attention was diverted from the three captives, which was probably exactly what Kismet intended with the message.

Contrary to popular belief, laser aiming devices were rarely used for long distance shooting, and when they were, they were almost always in infrared wavelengths, invisible without the aid of night vision goggles. The visible red dot lasers so common in movies and television shows were typically used only with handguns, and had an effective range of only about twenty-five yards, with the "dot" increasing in size as the beam dispersed over distance. At distances of more than a hundred yards, the illuminated area might be several feet across.

Maddock still wasn't convinced that there actually was a sniper, but in that moment, all that mattered to the magicians—Black and Aliyah included—was making sure that they weren't being targeted. It was just the distraction Maddock and Bones needed to seize the upper hand.

Both men exploded from their kneeling positions, easily overpowering and disarming the two would-be executioners. In a flash, both gunmen were on the ground, their pistols now pointed back at them. Jade surprised Black—and Maddock, as well—by deftly ducking away from the gun at her neck, and then twisting around in Black's grasp to ram her knee into his crotch so hard that even Bones let out a yelp of sympathetic pain.

Aliyah, unarmed and now outgunned, made an abortive attempt to flee, but only got as far as the nearest arch before a hand shot out to seize hold of her.

It was Nick Kismet, armed, not with a sniper rifle, but with his wicked-looking *kukri* knife, which he held in a saber grip, the tip just inches from Aliyah's eye.

"I warned you what would happen," he said, his voice low and menacing.

Aliyah tried to pull away, and when she failed at that, spat at him. "Go on. Kill me. Just as you killed my husband."

Kismet's expression changed, softened. He sighed and lowered the knife a few inches. "All right, you got me. I was bluffing. I never meant for your husband to die. He attacked me, I fought back, he fell. Call it self-defense or an accident. I didn't want to kill him, and don't want to kill you."

"Do you think I want your mercy?"

Kismet shook his head. "I don't care what you want. But if you keep this up, somebody is going to get hurt, and I guarantee it won't be me."

"Better believe him," advised Bones, with a chuckle. "You think you know magick? Trust me, you don't know diddly-squat."

"You have no idea what I know," Aliyah retorted.

Maddock wondered if the woman suspected the true meaning of Kismet's statement. Several years earlier, Kismet had been drawn into a quest for the secret of immortality—and he had found it. Now, not only did he look ten years younger than his actual age, but he could recover from even mortal injuries, healing completely in a matter of minutes. Maddock would not have believed it if he hadn't witnessed Kismet recover from a lethal jolt of electricity a few days earlier.

But even though Kismet was invulnerable, the rest of them weren't which was why the continued harassment from Aliyah's magicians was becoming a serious problem, particularly as they seemed all too eager to indulge in cold-blooded murder.

"Well," Kismet said lowering the knife further but keeping an unbreakable grip on the woman's arm. "It's a stalemate then. I can't allow you to keep coming after us, and since I'm not going to just kill you outright, that seems to leave only one option. You'll have to come with us."

"Now just hold on a second." Maddock's voice joined a chorus of protest. Everyone—from Jade and Rose to Black and the other magicians—had something to say about the suggestion.

Aliyah just eyed Kismet, warily. "You would do that? Knowing that I have sworn to destroy you."

Kismet shrugged. "I've been told I have a weakness for bad girls."

Aliyah's face twisted with revulsion. "In your dreams."

Maddock cleared his throat. "Nick, we can't trust her. First chance she gets, she'll turn on us. And even if she doesn't get that chance, we're not going to be able to travel with a hostage."

Kismet continued staring at Aliyah. "You don't have to be our hostage. Look, we both want to find the Emerald Tablet. We've already got three of the four elementals. That gives us an edge. But you know more about it than any of us. So, let's work together."

"And when we find it?"

"We cross that bridge when we come to it. Your best chance of ever seeing it is with us."

Maddock exchanged a look with Bones, who just shook his head. "Put a snake in your pocket, you're gonna get bit," he said, with an expansive air, as if reciting some bit of tribal lore.

"It's painful for me to say this," Jade said, keeping her eyes on Black, along with the business end of the pistol she'd taken from him, "but I agree with Bones. She's poison. We can't trust her."

Maddock shook his head. "No, Nick's right. We're not cold-blooded killers." He turned to Aliyah. "And we're not the only ones looking for it. It makes sense to work together."

"If you refuse," Kismet said, still staring at the woman, "or if they convince me that you can't be trusted, we'll drop you off somewhere. Probably out in the middle of nowhere, far from telephones and roads."

Aliyah's eyes narrowed again, but her expression lost some of its venom. "When you put it like that, how can I say no?"

6.

After depriving the magicians of the keys to their vehicles, along with all weapons and mobile communications devices, the team of five plus one, piled into their rented Toyota Land Cruiser and began the four-hour-long drive back to Ankara. Aliyah offered no resistance and showed no overt signs of treacherous intent; she even went as far as to instruct her men to return to Plymouth and await further instructions, though whether that was a sincere request or part of a pre-arranged ruse was anyone's guess. She seemed resigned to her situation, though Maddock wondered how much of that was due to the fact that she had at least two guns pointed at her the whole time.

An hour into the journey, while driving along the surprisingly modern D750 highway, which cut across the Anatolian Plateau and offered a spectacular view of the distant volcanic peak of Mount Hasan, Bones who was driving, glanced over his shoulder. "This seems as good a place as any. I'll slow down a little if you want to toss her out."

"Bones!" cried Rose from the shotgun seat. "That's not funny."

"I wasn't joking," Bones said, dead-pan. Then he reached up and tilted the rear-view mirror to adjust his view. "Or did you think I was talking about Jade?"

Jade, who had the middle row seats all to herself, pretended to scratch her nose with just her middle finger extended.

Ever the peacemaker, Rose unbuckled her seat belt and threaded her way back to the middle row. Kneeling on the seat next to Jade, she peered over the backrest at Aliyah, who sat in the rear seating area, bracketed by Maddock and Kismet. "You knew we weren't going to find the Emerald Tablet at Tyana."

Aliyah shrugged, not meeting Rose's stare. "Many have looked for it. If it was there to find, someone would have. But I wonder if it was ever there at all."

"You mean after Balinas originally found it?"

Aliyah now raised her head to look back at Rose, regarding her thoughtfully, as if trying to decide whether to trust her. "It may be that the story in the *Kitāb sirr al-ḫalīqa* is not a literal account of the discovery of the tablet."

The Persian name seemed to flow naturally off her lips, a gift of her exotic ancestry.

"An allegory?"

Aliyah shifted in her seat, ignoring the guns held by Maddock and Kismet. "Or a riddle."

Maddock now took an interest. "I like riddles."

Aliyah glanced over at him, then looked forward again. "Balinas, is also known by the name Pseudo-Apollonius of Tyana. This is the first part of the riddle."

Rose nodded. "The real Apollonius of Tyana lived in the First Century. He was a famous neo-Pythagorean philosopher and writer, though none of his original writings survive."

"He was more than that," Aliyah said firmly. "He was a magus. A semi-divine figure, traveling the world, teaching and performing miracles. Some believe his story was the inspiration for the Gospels."

"*The* Gospels?" Bones called out. "The Bible stories about Jesus?"

"Yes. There are many similarities. In fact, in the Second Century, those who followed the teachings of Apollonius believed that Jesus was a pale imitation of the sage. In any event, Balinas lived many centuries later, and may have chosen that appellation to give his own writings more import and broaden his reach.

"That was a common practice among Classical philosophers, riding the coattails of more famous men."

Bones nodded sagely. "Like all those guys who write novels and let James Patterson slap his name on the cover."

Aliyah made a sour face. "No, nothing like that. In this instance, I believe Balinas' alter-ego was offering a clue to the true origin of the Emerald Tablet."

"The real Apollonius?"

"Let's set that aside for a moment. Balinas

claimed the true author of the Emerald Tablet was Hermes Trismegistus—Hermes the Thrice-Great."

Maddock was becoming interested despite himself. "Rose told us about this. As Hellenistic culture spread across Egypt, the gods of both cultures blended together to form distinct new god-forms. Just as the Roman Jupiter is based on the Greek Zeus, Hermes Trismegistus was based on the Greek Hermes and the Egyptian god Thoth, but some of the Egyptian deities might have been men who were deified after death. It is generally believed that Thoth might have originally been the priest Imhotep—"

"The bad guy in The Mummy," Bones supplied.

"And the architect of the Step Pyramid," Rose said, with a roll of her eyes. "Thoth might also have been based on Amenhotep, son of Hapu. Hermes Trismegistus might have been an Egyptian magician and priest. A real person, not an abstract god."

Maddock snapped his fingers as inspiration dawned. "The Magus card!"

The Magus was the name assigned to a card in the Thoth Tarot deck designed by Aleister Crowley. Maddock and Kismet had found an early version of the card with the remains of Adam Garral, the occultist who had first discovered the Apex and an ancestor of Kismet's adoptive father. The card was itself another riddle, and an anachronism, as Crowley's Tarot deck had not been produced until more than thirty years after Garral's disappearance and death in the frozen wilderness of Antarctica.

Maddock leaned forward to look past Aliyah to Kismet. "The card has the figure of Mercury—the Roman version of Hermes. And Hermes is also Thoth. Three faces of Hermes—thrice-great—and all called the Magus, or Magician."

"The point," Aliyah said, her voice edged with irritation, "Is that Hermes and Hermes Trismegistus were never considered to be the same entity in the eyes of the Greeks, so it is unlikely that the Emerald Tablet written by one would have been concealed in a temple dedicated to the other."

"So we should be looking for a temple to Thoth?"

Aliyah appraised Maddock again for a moment, then seemed to relax a little. She turned to look at Kismet. "Do you recall your vision of the Emerald Tablet? You first saw it as an Egyptian sword—a *kopis*—the sword of Alexander the Great—concealed within the tower of Babel."

Kismet nodded. "It seemed that way."

"Alexander the Great spread Hellenistic culture across the world of his day—here, in what was once called Asia Minor and across the Persian world, but this influence was felt most strongly in one place. Egypt. And particularly in the city that bears his name to this day."

"Alexandria," Rose said, almost breathless. "The Library!"

She turned to look at Maddock. "Hermes and Thoth were both patron gods of the written word.

Thoth in particular was the god of wisdom. And libraries. And what better place to keep the Emerald Tablet than the Library of Alexandria."

"Balinas lived in the Eighth Century," Kismet countered. "The library was completely destroyed long before that."

"Contrary to popular belief," Rose said, slipping into history-professor mode, "the Library was not sacked and burned in a single event, but rather suffered numerous episodes of destruction, some intentional, others the result of accidents and natural disasters. Earthquakes and tsunamis did a lot of damage. Nobody knows exactly where the Library once stood. It was customary for ancient civilizations to salvage the stone and other material for use in other building projects, not to mention repurposing the real estate. There's a modern city where ancient Alexandria once stood, and as you can imagine, the current Arab populace isn't keen on having the streets of their city dug up for the sake of satisfying curiosity about the Western world."

"So how are we going to find it?" Bones asked.

"Well, we do have a few clues from history. For one thing, most of the historical accounts of the Library indicate that it was part of the royal palace complex. Now, we don't know exactly where that was either, but there have been a few hopeful discoveries. In 1992, a French archaeologist discovered the sunken remains of the royal quarters of Cleopatra VII—"

"Seven?" Bones interrupted. "There was more than one? Were they all babes?"

Rose laughed. "There were actually seven women named Cleopatra, but Cleo Seven was the famous one—the one that Julius Caesar and Mark Anthony were so enthralled with. I leave it to you to decide if the word 'babe' is accurate, but if the artwork from the time is any indication, she most definitely didn't look anything like Elizabeth Taylor in her prime. Plutarch says she was beautiful, but not extraordinarily so, and then goes on to praise her wit and charm. And especially her voice."

"Ah," Bones said, sounding a little disappointed. "A great personality and a face for radio."

Maddock tried to get the conversation back on track. "Her quarters would probably have been in the palace complex. You said its underwater?"

"About sixteen feet under," Rose said. "In the harbor, a couple hundred yards offshore."

"Well that's no problem then," Bones said, quickly getting over his disillusionment. "Underwater is where we do our best work."

"The bay is toxic," Aliyah said, calm and confident. "Poisoned with petroleum and industrial waste. But by all means, search underwater to your heart's content."

Maddock eyed her. "It's not underwater?"

"If I told you where to look, you would have no further use for me."

"Just knowing it's in Alexandria may be enough, as long as we've got the relics to guide us."

Aliyah shrugged. "I can tell you exactly where to look. Or you can take your chances. It's your choice."

"I say we take our chances," Bones said.

"Hold on a second," Jade said. "If you've known all along that it was there, why didn't you get it yourself?"

Aliyah kept looking at Kismet. "Until you saw the vision of the four elementals, we did not know what we were looking for. If we had suspected, we would have brought the Magna of Illusion here and opened the vault ourselves. Perhaps if you had not killed him, my husband would have been the one to behold the vision."

Anger had darkened her features as she spoke, but after a pause, her expression softened. "I told you in Plymouth, Nick Kismet. I believe you are meant to find it."

Kismet just stared back, stone-faced.

Maddock understood his wariness. Aliyah had set a trap for them in Tyana. Was she now trying to lead them into another?

7.

Alexandria, Egypt

Like many other cities Maddock had visited in his travels, Alexandria was a collision of past and present. The ancient past, what little of it remained, was like a granite bluff extending out into the ocean, slowly but inevitably eroding away under the relentless assault of progress.

There was plenty to remind visitors of the city's history, and indeed, tourism remained a major industry, despite recent political turmoil in the Arab world. But even though the ancient monuments, such as the misnamed Pompey's Pillar and the Catacombs of Kom El-Shouqafa, and more recent but no less historic structures—such as the Citadel of Qaitbay, which occupied the ground where the famed Pharos Lighthouse once stood, or the magnificent Mosque of Abu al-Abbas al-Mursi—continued to generate interest in the city, tourists now came as much for modern pleasures such as sunbathing and gambling, as for a deep interest in history. For many, the ancient ruins were a curiosity, on par with a modern theme park. Even the ancient Library of antiquity had been reimagined as a fantastic modern structure of glass and steel, surrounded by gardens and reflecting pools, perched at the eastern tip of the harbor.

Although its collection, which included not only millions of books but also film, video archives, and over 100 terabytes of data, was greater by several orders of magnitude than its namesake from antiquity, the Bibliotheca Alexandrina seemed like just another tourist attraction.

Their flight, from Cairo—a short hop after the longer trip across the Mediterranean—landed just as the sun was settling below the western horizon. Since the end of the road trip in Ankara, where they had been obliged to dump their captured weapons, Aliyah had ceased to be their prisoner and was now a traveling companion, evidently a willing one, though Bones continued to vocally register his suspicions about her. Maddock harbored the same doubts, but was a little surprised by his friend's unrelenting antipathy toward her. It wasn't like Bones to pass up a chance to make a fool of himself in front of an attractive woman, and by any standard, Aliyah was that.

They traveled by minibus to their hotel just a couple blocks from the harbor, but stayed in their rooms just long enough to offload their luggage, such as it was, and grab a quick meal in the hotel restaurant.

As they finished their supper over cups of coffee, Aliyah began revealing the knowledge she had earlier withheld, doling the information out like a tour guide. "The Library of Alexandria was originally part of a larger institution of learning and research on subjects ranging from philosophy to astronomy to anatomy. In addition to the enormous wealth of wisdom and knowledge contained on scrolls, the institution included laboratories, observatories, and even a zoo. It was dedicated to the nine Muses of Greek mythology—the deities who inspired the creative arts—from which it derived its name: Musaeum."

"And from which we get, museum," Maddock said.

"It's described as a campus with several buildings, connected by covered walkways, gardens, dining halls and dormitories, even a theatre. Oddly enough, the one thing that original museum didn't have was an art collection, but it was the start of the Library. By 145 BCE though, the center of learning in Alexandria shifted to another building, called the Serapeum—the temple of the Greco-Egyptian god Serapis, the protector deity of Alexandria."

"Greco-Egyptian," Maddock mused. "Like Hermes Trismegistus."

"Serapis was a syncretic deity—a joining of beliefs from different religions. The name derives from a combination of the Egyptian deities Osiris and Apis, but he seems to have a lot more in common with Dionysus. Interestingly, the *Anabasis Alexandri*, generally considered to be the best source for information about Alexander the Great, says that as Alexander lay dying of fever, his companions asked Serapis—which I would take to mean a statue of the god—whether to bring him into the temple to be cured. The account says that the god spoke and told them to leave Alexander where he was. Mind you, this was in Babylon, not Alexandria.

"In any case though, the Serapeum of Alexandria was the most famous temple to the god, not to mention being the most impressive temple in the whole city. As the Musaeum declined, the Serapeum not only grew in prominence, but housed at least part of the Library Collection—the part that survived the longest. There were however statues to all the Greek gods, including Hermes, in the Serapeum. Balinas might have lived in the Eighth Century, but Apollonius of Tyana lived in the First, so it stands to reason that if he visited Alexandria, he would have gone to the Serapeum."

"So what happened to the Serapeum?"

"When Emperor Constantine converted to Christianity in 325 C.E., he ordered the Serapeum closed, along with all other temples to pagan gods. The Alexandrians held out for a while, but in 391, the Serapeum was sacked. That's generally considered to be the end of the Library of Alexandria, though it's likely that at least some of the collection was preserved elsewhere. There's even one legend that part of it was loaded aboard a Roman galley which eventually wound up in Texas."

"Really?" Bones was now definitely paying attention.

"Probably not," Aliyah went on. "Arab sources attribute the final destruction to the order of the ruling Caliph, after Muslim forces captured the city in 642 C.E. but given the subsequent Golden Age of Islam, in which science and mathematics continued to evolve throughout the period known in Europe as 'the Dark Ages,' it is likely they preserved the knowledge, rather than destroying it. After the Library of Alexandria, the greatest library in history was in the Persian fortress of Alamut."

"The seat of power for the famed Hashashin—the Assassins cult," Rose said, nodding. "My great grandad wrote about it one of the Dodge Dalton novels."

Aliyah gave a disdainful sniff, then continued, "The Serapeum is gone but we know where it once stood.

"In 297 C.E., Emperor Diocletian erected a triumphal column at the Serapeum. A granite monolith carved from a single stone, rather than stacked drums, over sixty feet high, and it's still standing today. If you read the tourist brochures, you know it as 'Pompey's Pillar' though in fact it has nothing to do with Pompey the Great who once ruled Rome alongside Julius Caesar. The foundation of the Serapeum lies nearby, along with the entrance to the Catacombs of Kom El-Shouqafa. I believe we will find the vault with the Tabula Smaragdina within those ancient tunnels."

"Unless someone took it when they relocated the rest of the Library."

"I do not believe that happened." Aliyah turned to Kismet. "Do you recall the story of how Adam

Garral found the Apex in the Great Pyramid?"

Kismet had been unusually subdued since their arrival. During the taxi ride, Maddock had observed him looking around warily, as if checking to see if they were being tailed. When he had asked Kismet about it, the man had simply replied. "I don't like the desert." Now, he straightened in his chair and nodded. "He claimed it appeared to him after some kind of out-of-body experience."

"In which he found a secret passage inside the pyramid. A passage that not only led to a secret room, but transported him through time as well. Balinas describes a similar journey into the vault under the statue of Hermes to find the Emerald Tablet. And unlike your ancestor, he did not remove what he found."

"It could still be there," said Maddock.

"With the relics you now carry, we will find that vault. It will open to us, even as it did for Apollonius of Tyana, and inside we will find the tomb of Alexander the Great and in his hand, the Emerald Tablet of Hermes Trismegistus." She pushed her empty coffee cup away. "Are you ready?"

"You mean right now?" Maddock glanced around the table and saw his look of concern mirrored in the faces of the others. "It's dark out."

"Meaning we will not be disturbed by other visitors." Aliyah folded her arms across her chest. "I expected a little more enthusiasm."

"I don't like to rush into things," Maddock said. He half-expected Bones to make a joke at his expense, but the big Cherokee just nodded.

"Well, she's got a point about not being bothered by the tourists," Jade said, though she sounded almost like she was trying to convince herself. "We can at least check the place out."

Rose seconded the suggestion. "Judging by the reaction we got in Antarctica and on Drake Island, we should be able to tell if it's there just by walking by."

Aliyah stared at the other women intently but said nothing. Maddock shot a look at Kismet, who simply shrugged. "I guess it wouldn't hurt to do a walk-by."

Although it was not required by local custom, Aliyah suggested the women wear *hijab* headscarves to avoid attracting unnecessary attention. As Jade and Rose donned their scarves, Aliyah glanced at Bones and added, "I'm afraid there's not much we can do to cover him up."

"What the hell is that supposed to mean?"

"Only that you stand out in a crowd," she replied with a coy smile.

That mollified Bones somewhat. "It's true. I am outstanding."

"Well since you've got the best view," Maddock said, "keep that head on a swivel."

He glanced over at Kismet who returned a nod of confirmation. This all felt too rushed, like a trap, but even if it was, there was no way around it. They could either go through, or go home.

As promised, the former site of the Serapeum was only a few blocks from the hotel. The surrounding neighborhood was quiet and poorly lit. All six of them stood out, though Bones perhaps more than the others, attracting the notice of more than a few *jellabiya*-clad local men, all of whom looked away quickly when Bones gave them the stink-eye.

Aliyah took them along the edge of a rocky plateau occupying several acres where no modern construction had taken place. "This is the old Bab Sidra cemetery," she explained, and pointed forward to the column, a dark silhouette thrust up into the night sky, perhaps a quarter of a mile distant. "That is where we must go."

Maddock maintained his 360-degree awareness as they moved along the edge of the cemetery, occasionally checking with Bones and Kismet to see if they had noticed anything of concern. Maddock was pleased to see that Jade also remained alert. She had, he realized, come a long way from the hapless, trouble-prone archaeologist he had rescued from a submerged ruin in Argentina all those years before. *Probably Professor's influence*, he thought. *Definitely not the girl I fell out of love with.*

The thought went through his head—and the rest of him—before he knew what was happening.

Cut it out, Maddock. He told himself, forcefully. *You've got Angel, and she's all the woman you'll ever need.*

He forced his gaze forward again as they came to the gate that blocked access to the ruins. It was closed and secured with a padlock.

"Guess we'll have to come back tomorrow," Bones said. "Oh, well. We tried."

Although the fabric of her *hijab* hid her hair, Aliyah's exposed eyebrows went up in an expression of surprise, or perhaps dismay. "I would not have thought men such as yourselves would be stopped by something so primitive."

Bones glanced over at Maddock in a "what do you think?" look. Maddock could only shrug.

Bones let out a sigh. "Challenge accepted," he said, and reached into a pocket for his lockpicking tools. "My misspent youth pays off again."

With one hand cupped over the screen of his mobile phone for light, Bones went to work on the lock. Rose moved closer to Maddock. "Dane, I'm not getting anything."

She had whispered it, but Aliyah overheard nonetheless. "The relics are not reacting?" There was no hint of coy playfulness now; her surprise was real. "I don't understand."

"Same with the Apex," Kismet said, absently fingering the talisman which hung from a rawhide cord around his neck. "Nada."

"Maybe we aren't close enough," Maddock suggested.

"We got a reaction from the orb from miles away," Rose countered.

"You have three relics now, correct?" Aliyah said. "Perhaps they are setting up an interference pattern. Canceling each other out."

The suggestion felt sincere, but Maddock couldn't help but wonder if this was the prelude to a betrayal. Was Aliyah trying to get them to separate? Isolate the relics and divide their forces?

"That didn't happen on Drake Island," Rose said. Nevertheless, she unslung the backpack, opening it to begin rooting around inside.

"Got it," Bones said as he removed the lock from the hasp. He started to pull the gate open but stopped himself. "Or should I lock it back up?"

"At least walk around," Aliyah pleaded. "It has to be here. Maybe you just need to be closer."

Maddock looked to Kismet for some hint of what to do. The latter shook his head. "I think this is another dead end. But we're here. We might as well try it." He fixed Aliyah with a cold stare. "It's not like we're completely defenseless."

Aliyah tilted her head in a gesture that indicated she understood the implicit threat, and then reached for the gate. She swung it open and went through without waiting for them.

There was just enough ambient light for them to make out the path winding through the ruins. They passed excavations and mounds, eventually reaching the crest of the hill where Pompey's Pillar stood, its enormous base flanked by a pair of sphinx statues, each the size of a bull elephant. Aliyah led them past the column, following a route that she seemed to have memorized, and brought them to a large hole in the ground.

Maddock activated the flashlight on his phone but kept one hand over it to mute the light and mask their presence. He shone it into the hole, revealing a staircase of cut stone that descended into the gloom. Round shapes, like black ping-pong ball halves, skittered away from the touch of his light.

"Scarab beetles," Bones murmured. "Don't let them get under your skin."

"This is the entrance to the old tunnel system that once connected the temples of the Serapeum," Aliyah explained. After a momentary pause, she turned to Rose. "Has there been any reaction from the elemental relics?"

Rose shook her head.

"I don't understand," Aliyah said, her voice becoming increasingly taut. "It has to be here. You must be doing something wrong."

"I'm not *doing* anything," Rose protested. "And neither is the orb. There's nothing—"

Before Rose could finish, Aliyah sprang into motion, seizing Rose's backpack strap. Maddock started to react, but Aliyah was already moving, dragging Rose into the dark hole.

8.

Maddock unhooded his light and shone it down the steps, catching just a glimpse of Rose as she stumbled along behind Aliyah. Then he was moving, too, pounding down the steps in pursuit. He felt more than heard the crunch of beetle bodies underfoot and some part of him recalled Bones' warning about the scarabs getting under his skin. That was a silly notion, he knew, a nightmare fantasy straight out of a B-movie. The Egyptian scarab was actually a dung-beetle, not a flesh eater at all. But telling himself that and believing it were two very different things, especially here, on the cusp of an ancient Egyptian catacomb. He could feel tiny insect legs crawling on his skin, mandibles clicking… Burrowing.

Crunch. Crunch.

The steps fed into a narrow tunnel and again he spied something moving in the darkness ahead. He did not stop, but in that moment of transition, he realized that the others were with him. Kismet was right beside him, and Jade and Bones weren't far behind.

Maddock skidded to a stop as his light fell upon a familiar form, lying sprawled on the passage floor, one hand raised to provide shade from the glare of the light. It was Rose. She looked a little disoriented but did not appear to be injured. There was no sign

WOOD AND ELLIS | 99

of Aliyah, though Maddock thought he heard the crunching sound of footsteps from further down the passage.

"She took my pack," Rose gasped. "She has the orb. And the mirror."

"We'll get them back," Maddock promised, helping her to her feet. He tried to inject a little confidence into his tone, though deep down, he wasn't feeling it. Aliyah now possessed two of the four elemental relics, and if she was right and the last remaining one lay somewhere in the catacombs beneath the Serapeum, then odds were good that she would soon have three.

Then Bones gave them all something else to worry about. "Holy crap. Scorpion."

Maddock followed Bones' pointing finger and saw something crawling up the outside of Rose's thigh. It was three inches in length, with a greenish-yellow segmented body, yellow legs, and a curled bobbing tail.

"A deathstalker," Kismet warned, unsheathing his *kukri*. "Don't move, Rose."

He extended the tip toward Rose's leg, placing the flat of the blade in the scorpion's path. It stopped moving, its forelegs resting a fraction of an inch from the edge, as if somehow sensing the potential lethality of the metal.

"Get it off me," Rose wailed.

"Don't move," Kismet repeated, and then with a snap of his wrist, flicked the creature away. "Dane, check her for more."

Rose was already moving, retreating back toward the stairs, her limbs twitching with the involuntary reflex known colloquially as the heebie-jeebies.

"Hold still, Rose." Maddock played his light up and down her body, and when he was satisfied that there were no other scorpions or any other creepy crawlies on her, turned and shone the light on the walls and ceiling of the passage. He saw more of the scarabs, roving aimlessly across the floor, but there were also several lighter-colored shapes.

"Deathstalker," Jade said. "Cute name." There was a faint quaver in her voice that might have been merely the result of the sprint down the stairs, but probably wasn't. She was also backing slowly toward the stairs.

Maddock had heard of the deathstalker scorpion. Despite the ominous name, its venom wasn't automatically fatal, particularly to a healthy adult and in the amount that might be delivered by a single creature, but a sting would be immediately painful, much like a bee sting, and as with bee stings, there was always the risk of a potentially fatal allergic reaction.

Unfortunately, there wasn't just one of the creatures, but dozens. Perhaps even hundreds of them, just in the area revealed by the light.

"Did I mention that I hate the desert?" Kismet said, more resigned than fearful. He continued to hold his *kukri* in his right hand.

"Right?" Bones said. "First scarabs, and now scorpions. It's like someone took all the worst parts of the Mummy movies and dumped them down here. I don't even want to think about what other horrible things might be waiting for us down there."

"Like Brendan Fraser," Jade said.

"Hey, I like Brendan Fraser," Bones shot back. "Though, I like young Rachel Weisz even more."

"Tom Cruise then?"

"We do not speak of that," Bones said, flatly.

"We need to keep moving," Maddock said, taking a step forward. He kept moving the light back and forth, up and down, making sure to avoid walking directly under any of the scorpions, or letting any of them get close enough to crawl onto his boots. After a few steps he glanced back and was relieved to see that the others were following.

Aliyah had left a clear trail for them to follow—crushed beetle carapaces and smeared bug guts stamped on the floor of the passage in distinctive footprint shapes. Not that there were a lot of places she could have gone. The tunnel continued forward for a ways before making a right turn and then another, but there were no branching passages. A hundred strides brought them to another descending staircase.

Maddock paused at the top, cocking an ear toward the unplumbed depths below and listened. The soft thud of footsteps echoed up from below.

Aliyah was still on the move. Maddock started down after her.

After just a few steps, the wall to his right fell away to reveal an open space beyond, a yawning emptiness into which the scant illumination of his flashlight vanished entirely. Thankfully, there were no more creepy-crawly denizens in evidence. Maddock shied away from the edge, hugging the left wall, which he absently noted slanted as it rose toward the ever-diminishing ceiling. The wall appeared to be constructed of stacked stone blocks or bricks, all of them adorned in some way, either with relief carvings of Egyptian hieroglyphs or some kind of alphabetic writing that Maddock guessed was probably Greek. He didn't take the time to stop and look.

"Dane!" Kismet called out to him in a stage whisper. "We're in a pyramid."

The significance of this was not immediately apparent to Maddock, or it seemed, to Bones, who shot back, "So?"

"So, there aren't any pyramids in Alexandria."

"He's right," Rose said. "At least none that have been discovered."

Maddock faltered a step as he processed this, then started moving again. "So, this is some kind of secret chamber?"

"One that Aliyah opened," Kismet replied. "Using the relics. I don't know if she did it consciously, or if the entrance simply reacted to their presence."

"Then she was right. The Emerald Tablet is here." Maddock quickened his pace.

"If it is, then it's not behaving like the other relics. I'm not getting any kind of reaction from the Apex."

The stairwell flattened onto a corner landing where the slanted wall met another just like it, apparently confirming Kismet's assessment. The stairs continued downward to the right, the number of steps half-again as many as the first flight and then turned right again, describing a square clockwise spiral down the interior walls of the hollow pyramid.

And then, the steps ended, depositing them on a broad stone pavement. The space was empty, devoid of even dust, but Maddock could just make out a trail of faint footprints leading out toward what he guessed to be the center. Holding his light high, he sprinted out across the flat, featureless floor in pursuit of Aliyah. Fifty yards or so later, he spotted her.

Whether by accident or design Maddock could not say, but Aliyah had somehow managed to find the only object contained within the pyramid—a block of stone, shaped like a rectangular prism, about four feet high and six feet long, and positioned, if Maddock was not mistaken, directly in the center of the chamber. A funerary bier, Maddock guessed, where a coffin—perhaps the golden coffin of Alexander the Great himself—had once lain. But the only thing on the bier now was

Aliyah Cerulean. She had fallen across it, and now lay face down with her arms outflung, hugging the stone. She looked like a grieving widow who had thrown herself upon the coffin of her deceased beloved, only there was no coffin. Rose's backpack lay on the floor beside her, unopened. Forgotten.

"Not here," she said, her voice hollow, desolate. "It's not here."

Maddock hastened forward to remove the backpack from her vicinity, though it was apparent that Aliyah either had no intention of using the relics or lacked the ability. Only then did he acknowledge what she had said.

"It's not here?"

Kismet and Bones were already there with him, and Rose and Jade arrived seconds later, spreading out in a loose circle around the stone block. Bones asked the obvious question. "What happened to it?"

"Someone else got here first," Kismet said, a hint of bitterness in his tone. "It was foolish of us to think that it would still be here."

"Who?"

"Who do you think?" The voice, a sardonic almost-shout, echoed and rebounded from the inwardly slanting walls. It had not come from anyone in their group, but despite the weird acoustical distortion, Maddock recognized it instantly. A chill of dread shot through him.

The voice belonged to the man he had dubbed TBH, owing to the latter's annoying habit of utilizing text-shorthand in everyday speech.

Maddock had tangled with the man on at least two previous occasions—first, in the Antarctic Outpost where they had discovered the orb, and then again in Plymouth Harbor, shortly after capturing the Magna of Illusion from Aliyah's brotherhood of magicians—and both encounters had ended the same way. Both times, Maddock had killed TBH.

It was only after the second encounter that Maddock had learned the truth about TBH—also known as Ulrich Hauser. The man was the leader of a radical splinter faction inside the secretive group known as Prometheus.

He was also Nick Kismet's brother, and like Kismet, Ulrich Hauser was, for all intents and purposes, immortal.

9.

Every head but Aliyah's whirled around to face back toward the stairs and the source of the voice. Something was moving there, a lot of somethings.

It might have been only his imagination, but Maddock thought he could see dozens of shadowy forms spreading out in either direction, just beyond the faint reach of their combined lights. Hauser, he knew, never went anywhere without a coterie of hired killers and this time would be no exception.

"Nobody move," Maddock whispered, unnecessarily. His friends were all still as statues.

The man himself materialized a moment later, stepping into the light. His face was partly concealed behind a set of night vision goggles, but after just a few steps toward the group, he flipped the low-light device up out of the way to completely reveal his grinning visage.

"Curious advice, Mr. Maddock. Moving targets are so much harder to hit."

Maddock shrugged. "I've killed you twice already. Maybe the third time is the charm."

It wasn't completely false bravado. He and Bones had been in stickier situations, although at that moment, he was hard-pressed to remember any, but the one thing experience had taught him was that there was absolutely no value to treating any situation as hopeless.

Hauser gave a short humorless laugh. Despite his strong handsome proportions, the man looked cruel and predatory—part-Adonis, part-werewolf. He closed to within ten feet of them, and then stopped with his hands resting on his hips. He regarded them all for a moment, one by one, his stare sharpening into daggers of hate as he met Maddock's stare, then he brought his gaze back to Kismet. "Surprised to see me, brother?"

"Not really." He thrust his chin at Hauser. "Frankly, I'm a little surprised it took you this long to bounce back after getting your ass handed to you back at Plymouth."

Bones gave a snort of laughter. "Nice."

Hauser shrugged. "I was otherwise occupied. I knew you'd end up here eventually." He paused a beat. "Well? Have you figured it out yet?"

Kismet's expression twitched a little. "I'm not really in the mood for guessing games."

Hauser's grin deepened. "Oh, but this one is the best. Maybe your new friends can help." He glanced at Maddock, his nostrils flaring angrily. "Interesting company you're keeping, BTW."

Bones let out an audible groan. "This again? Oh, wait. I've got one. FWIW, you're a dick."

Hauser ignored the jibe and returned his attention to Kismet. "A hint then." He made an expansive gesture. "The lost tomb of Alexander the Great, hidden away for at least two thousand years. Locked up tight, and the only keys that can open it are the four anomalies one of which was sealed within. What does that tell you?"

Maddock, curious despite himself, considered Hauser's question, but Kismet merely shrugged. "That someone else got here first. We already knew that."

"Ah, but how? Look around you. This place has been cleaned out, and yet there are no tunnels. This wasn't the work of tomb robbers. Whoever did this knew how to unlock the door and then seal it up again."

"They didn't use the orb," Rose said. There was a quiet defiance in her tone.

"I'd say the mirror is out, too," Jade added, jerking a thumb in Aliyah's direction. "Her magicians had the mirror this whole time and didn't even know there was anything here."

Hauser nodded, still looking at Kismet. "Which just leaves your little bauble. The Garral family heirloom."

Kismet cocked his head sideways. "You think Adam Garral took it?"

"That makes sense," Maddock said, thinking out loud. "Garral had the Apex and he probably had access to the mirror. We know he was looking for the orb. Maybe he came here first."

"But what did he do with it?" countered Rose. "Where is it now?"

Hauser continued smiling. "I like the way you think," he said, sounding like some kind of nightmarish motivational speaker. "But you jumped to the wrong conclusion. If Adam Garral had found

Alexander's tomb, believe me, the world would know about it."

Kismet looked up sharply. "Prometheus."

Hauser nodded. "Did you never think to ask, of all the people in the world, why our dear mother chose to leave you with Christian Garral."

Kismet just stared back, dumbfounded. Maddock suddenly felt like an intruder in the other man's family drama. If not for the guns he knew were pointed at them at all, he would have excused himself. But like it or not, he was already caught in the conflict.

"Prometheus wanted the Apex," he said, still trying to work it out for himself. "And they knew Christian Garral had it."

Hauser bobbed his head from side to side in a vague nod but kept his eyes on Kismet. "They wanted what it would unlock. This. The tomb of Alexander and all its secrets. The fourth anomaly was only a very small part of what was once kept here. Once the door was open and the treasures removed, our mother returned the heirloom to your adoptive father."

He paused a beat. "It's always the long game with the old guard. Always an experiment. If they had wanted the Apex anomaly, they would simply have taken it, but they were content to let Garral keep it. I suspect they wanted to observe how you would interact with it."

Kismet kept staring a few seconds longer then shook his head as if waking up. "If you already had the Emerald Tablet, why come after—"

"But I don't have it," Hauser hissed, cutting him off. "Those fools buried it away, just like they bury everything. The power to reshape the world… Reshape reality itself, and what do they do with it? Put it on a shelf where no one can reach."

"That's why you want the elementals," Rose said. "You're going to war with Prometheus."

For the first time since stepping into the light, Hauser's smile became genuine. "The Antarctic anomaly would have sufficed to accomplish my plan, but with three anomalies, nothing will stand in my way."

"Just one little problem with that," Kismet said, straightening a little. "You don't have three anomalies. In fact, by my count, you don't have any."

"Threats, brother?" Hauser shook his head sadly. "Are you sure that's how you want this to go?"

"Violence seems to be the only language you speak."

"That, and textese," Bones added.

"And yet," Hauser countered, "You are all still very much alive."

"No thanks to you," Jade put in.

"Oh, but it is entirely thanks to me," Hauser retorted. "At this moment there are a half-dozen assault rifles trained on you—on all of you—"

"This seems familiar somehow," Bones muttered.

"I underestimated you and your friends in the past. I won't make that mistake again. If you show even the slightest hint of resistance, my men will open fire. That won't pose much of a problem for you and I, dear brother, but I think your friends will not fare so well. If I wanted you dead, we wouldn't be talking right now."

"So why are we still talking?" Kismet asked, sounding genuinely curious rather than defiant.

"Understand this, brother. I am going to take the three anomalies in your possession. There's nothing you can do to stop me. Whether I take them over the dead bodies of your friends is up to you."

"Me?"

Hauser took a step closer and then reached out to clasp Kismet's shoulder. "We're brothers, Nick. They took that from us. *She* took that from us. Kept us apart and in the dark, all for the sake of their great experiment. Doesn't that gall you?"

"So, this is about revenge? Against our mother? Against Prometheus?"

"Not revenge. It's about taking what is ours. Our birthright, brother." He gave Kismet's shoulder and emphatic shake. "They set us against each other from the beginning, cast us as rivals in their little drama. Cain and Abel. Jacob and Esau. Romulus and Remus. When all the while, we ought to have been Castor and Pollux. Brothers, fighting side by side, seizing control of our destiny and taking what we are owed. That is what I'm offering you brother."

"Offering me?"

Hauser let go and took a step back. "Come with me, and I'll let them live."

Before Kismet could answer, Aliyah raised her head and let out a wail of dismay. "No. You must not." She pushed away from the bier and threw herself at Maddock, grasping the strap of Rose's pack in another attempt to tear it away. Despite her ferocity and the swiftness with which she had acted, Maddock's fingers curled tight on the straps, refusing to give it up.

"No!" Aliyah shouted again, giving the pack a futile shake. Then, still holding on with her left hand, she raised her eyes and her right hand, index and middle fingers extended, and spoke again in a low voice that seemed to vibrate in the still air.

"*A'teh!*"

Her hand came down quickly in a straight line to point at the pavement. "*Mal'kut!*"

Maddock didn't recognize the strange language, but he intuitively grasped that Aliyah was attempting some kind of magickal ritual, perhaps trying to unleash the power of the relics.

Can she do that?

Her hand came up until it was level with her heart and then moved out to her right shoulder. "*Ve Gev—*"

The incantation was silenced by a thunderous report. Maddock felt another hard yank on the pack strap as Aliyah Cerulean jerked backward, almost lifted off her feet by the impact of a bullet. A spray of blood misted the bier behind her and then she crashed down atop it once more, this time on her back in a supine position, like an offering on an altar.

Maddock tore his gaze from her and looked back at Hauser, who now held a smoking semi-automatic pistol in his extended right arm. The fierce predatory grin was back. "We'll have none of that," he said, and then swung the muzzle toward Maddock, reaching out his left hand, palm open. "Give me that pack. Now."

Before Maddock could even think about what his response would be, Kismet stepped in front of the gun, hands raised in a show of surrender. "Don't," he said, imploring. "I'll go with you."

He turned back to face Maddock and reached out for the pack.

"Stop!" Hauser barked. He moved around Kismet, keeping the gun trained on Maddock. "Sorry, brother, but you're already too close for my comfort. Back up now, or my men will open fire."

Kismet held his ground a moment longer. "Give me your word. No one else dies."

Hauser inclined his head. "If that's what it takes."

Kismet took a step back. "Give them up, Dane."

"He's going to kill us all anyway," Jade hissed.

Kismet held Hauser's stare. "No, he's not."

Maddock hesitated. His gut told him that Jade

was right and that giving up the relics would only seal their death warrant, but at the same time, what choice did they have? Or was this some bold gambit on Kismet's part?

"Trust me, Dane," Kismet said. "This is the only way."

Maddock looked over at Bones, saw the mixture of disbelief and anger in his friend's eyes, read the unasked question there. *Are we really doing this?*

But Kismet was right. They were out of options. With no better alternative, Maddock knelt and placed the pack on the floor.

Hauser moved in quickly, snatching the pack up off the floor, and then darted back out of Maddock's reach. "That's better," he said, hefting the pack onto one shoulder. He waggled the gun at Maddock. "All right. All of you, move closer."

Kismet spoke quickly. "I swear, if you hurt them—"

"They are as insignificant to me as insects on the sidewalk." Hauser gave the pack a meaningful shake. "Especially now that I have these. But I won't tolerate further interference. Or delay. Maddock, do yourself a favor and make sure I never see your face again." He turned back to Kismet and gestured into the darkness. "It's time to go, brother. We have business elsewhere."

10.

As Kismet and Hauser melted into the shadows, Maddock shook off the paralysis of defeat and moved to the bier. He knew, even without checking for a pulse, that Aliyah was dead, but he checked anyway and then raised his eyes to the others and shook his head.

Bones nostrils flared in a feral snarl. "And I was actually starting to like that guy."

"Who?" Rose asked.

"Kismet. I didn't think he'd cut and run at the first sign of trouble."

"He didn't exactly have much of a choice," Jade said, defensively.

"Please." Bones waved a dismissive hand. "He could have used the relics, put the whammy on 'em. He didn't."

"Because he knew Hauser would probably kill us all before he could. He did the only thing he could. He bought us time. And a chance." She turned to Maddock. "We are going after them, right?"

Maddock just blinked.

"Dane?"

He finally allowed his eyes to focus. "And do what, Jade?"

Jade's eyebrows creased in a frown. "Stop Hauser," she said, as if the answer was obvious. "Get those relics back."

"How? The relics were the only thing that gave us an edge. Without them…" He shrugged. "Like he said, we're bugs on the sidewalk."

Jade had no answer to that, but Rose did. "Then we make our own luck, just like my great-grandad did when he first went to the Outpost."

Maddock managed a tight smile. "I guess I'll have to read those Dodge Dalton books when we get out of here."

"Getting out of here might be a good place to start," Bones remarked.

Maddock gazed out into the darkness. There was no sign of Hauser or his gunmen, no way of knowing if they were still there or already long gone. Hauser's final warning still echoed in his ears, but they couldn't remain where they were indefinitely. "All right. But let's take it slow. I don't want to give Hauser any reason to change his mind."

One day, you *will understand….*

Twenty-six years later, the words still haunted Nick Kismet. The words, and the horror that had preceded them.

One day, you will understand what we have done, and why it had to be done.

Nearly three decades of searching, had brought him no closer to understanding.

Despite the appearance of filial familiarity, Kismet and Hauser had only crossed paths on two previous occasions. That first meeting was the one that stuck in his memory.

In the early hours of what history now called the first Gulf War—a U.S. led coalition to turn back Saddam Hussein's invasion of Kuwait—Kismet, at the time, an Army Intelligence officer, had been sent behind enemy lines, accompanied by a squad of Ghurkas, purportedly to rescue a highly-placed Iraqi defector—a defector who had managed to steal one of the most famous artifacts in history from the secret vaults of the Iraqi national museum. And that was when Ulrich Hauser and Prometheus had stepped into his life, and everything had changed.

Yet, while he had spent the subsequent years trying to learn the truth about Prometheus, it was the memory of what Hauser had done in the moments before making that promise—

One day....

—that filled Kismet with dread.

Hauser had brutally, cold-bloodedly, murdered the Iraqi defector and his entire family.

One day, you will understand what we have done, and why it had to be done.

Kismet didn't understand, and didn't think he ever really would, but he did know what Hauser was capable of. Dane Maddock probably had no idea how narrowly he and the others had avoided the same fate.

As he trudged up the stairs behind Hauser, the way ahead dimly illuminated by the pale green glow of the chem-lights that dangled from tactical vests worn by Hauser and his men his only goal was to put some distance between Hauser and his new friends. He didn't dare lift a finger against his brother until he knew that Maddock and the others were safe.

Shortly after leaving the stairwell and re-entering the maze of passages outside the pyramid, Kismet heard a dull rumbling sound coming from behind them. He turned around, glimpsed something moving, but only for a moment. Then all was still. He squinted into the darkness but all he could see was a featureless stone wall.

The entrance to the passage had just closed.

He whirled around and shouted into the gloom. "Sealing them in wasn't part of the deal. If you want my help, you better leave the door open."

Hauser's reply drifted back to him from further up the tunnel. "It was nothing I did, brother. If I had to guess, I'd say the passage reacts when one of the anomalies is brought into close proximity. Or when they're removed. I can't very well leave any of them here and time is fleeting. But don't worry. Your new friends will be safe down there for at least a day or two. Long enough for us to finish our business."

Kismet knew any further pleas would be futile. And there was a silver lining; although they had only met a few days previously, Dane Maddock didn't seem like the sort of person to just give up and go home. Given the chance, he would come after Hauser.

And probably get himself killed.

He stalked ahead, catching up to Hauser just as the latter ascended the last set of steps back to the surface. "And what exactly is your plan?"

Without breaking stride, Hauser pulled off his night vision goggles and stashed them in the backpack with the elemental relics. The Apex had been added to the collection, along with Kismet's *kukri*. Hauser's men hastened ahead, presumably to make sure the way was clear. "Oh, it's quite simple. We're going to storm heaven and cast the gods down from their thrones."

"Is that supposed to mean something to me?"

Hauser chuckled. "I forget sometimes how little they've allowed you to know. The vault where the collection is kept is code-named Olympus. Where the gods reside." He resumed walking, following the path through the ruins toward the entrance gate. "Once we're in control of Olympus, nobody will be able to oppose us."

"Where is it?"

Hauser chuckled. "It's embarrassing but, TBH, I don't actually know. That's something I was hoping you could help me with."

"Me?" Kismet couldn't help but shake his head. "You're the insider."

"Alas, the location of the vault was the one secret I was never made privy to. I think they were afraid of what I might do if I had direct access to it. Which, I suppose, was wisdom on their part."

"Well they sure as hell didn't tell me."

Hauser said nothing until they reached the open gate. Through it, Kismet saw a line of waiting luxury full-sized sport utility vehicles, surrounded by even more armed commandos deployed in a strategic perimeter.

"While you and Maddock were spinning your wheels in Turkey," Hauser said, "I was busy finding the one person who can tell us where to find the vault. She hasn't told me where it is yet, but eventually she will." He strode to the closest vehicle and gripped the door handle. "I can afford to be patient, but your friends in Alexander's tomb won't have that luxury. I seem to recall that you were an interrogator, once upon a time. Maybe you can get her to talk."

He opened the door, revealing the lone passenger in the spacious interior of the SUV. A woman, late-middle-aged, long straight black hair shot through with gray, framing an olive complexion that, despite a tracery of wrinkles, remained beautiful by almost any standard. Kismet had never seen the woman before, but knew her instantly.

His mother.

"Crap," Bones snarled, kicking the wall that now blocked the stairwell. "Dead end."

Maddock moved closer and shone the light from

his phone onto the wall which slanted toward his head, another interior wall of the hollow pyramid. There was no sign of the passage through which they had entered; it seemed to have been erased from the very fabric of reality. "I was afraid something like this might happen," he admitted.

Bones cast an irritated frown at him. "'Let's take it slow,'" he said in a mocking falsetto which Maddock could only assume was meant to be an attempt at mimicking his own voice.

A poor attempt.

"Sorry," Maddock said, disingenuously. "I thought dealing with a potential closed door would be easier than surviving a hail of bullets. Clearly, I wasn't thinking straight."

"Whoa." Bones threw up his hands in an overly-dramatic defensive gesture. "Be careful where you point that sarcasm. You haven't been properly schooled in its use."

Jade laughed, probably enjoying the rare moment of discord between the two friends, but Rose was quick to intervene. "Can we save the recriminations for later? Like when we're out of here?"

"Why wait?" Bones countered. "We're probably gonna be here a while."

"There's got to be a way through," Maddock said, trying to take Rose's admonition to heart as he continued searching. "If there's a way to move this wall, I don't know what it is. But it looks like it's made of stacked stone blocks. If we can knock one loose, we should be able to break through. We just need something to use as a battering ram."

"We could use Bones' head," Jade suggested. "It's hard enough to smash stone."

"If you think my head is hard—"

"Bones!" Rose said, almost shrieking. "Enough." She stepped closer to Maddock and held something out to him. "Will this help?"

Maddock looked down at the wedge-shaped object she was holding and felt a glimmer of hope. It was the adamantine-infused hatchet head they had recovered from the plane wreck off the South Africa coast. "How did you manage to hang onto that?"

She grinned and shrugged a little. "When Aliyah mentioned that the relics might be causing an interference pattern, I took it out to see if it was still affected. Then I shoved it in my back pocket."

"Has it got any magic power left?" Bones asked, looking over Maddock's shoulder.

Rose waved the axe head back and forth in front of the wall, then brought it forward until metal and stone were in contact. Nothing happened.

"It was worth a shot," Bones muttered. "Now what?"

"Magic or not, it's still a metal tool," Maddock said, reaching out for the tomahawk. He took it from Rose and started tracing the seams with the spike on the back end.

"You actually think you can dig us out with that?" Jade asked, skeptically.

"If you've got a better idea, I'm all ears."

"Hey, if guys can tunnel out of Alcatraz using a spoon," Bones said, "I think we can manage this."

"I feel like you just made that up," Jade retorted, then added a little wistfully, "I wish Professor was here. He'd know."

Maddock exerted a little more pressure on the blade as he dragged it along the seam, and the resulting noise silenced further debate. He was surprised and heartened to see a long groove trailing out behind the point. The metal had scored the old stone as if it were as soft as chalk. Encouraged by this result, he shifted his grip on the tomahawk, holding it like an icepick, and drove the point forward in a hammer blow.

It was a mistake, or at least it seemed that way to him for a few seconds.

There was a bright flash on impact—friction sparks, he guessed—and a throb of pain that shot up his arm all the way to the shoulder. He felt as if he had just touched a live wire. The sensation quickly dulled to a tingle of pins and needles as his overloaded nerves went into shut down mode. The axe head fell from his numb fingers and clattered on the floor, lost from his view in the subsequent eruption of fine rock dust the strike had caused. It was only when the dust began to settle that he saw the need to revise his opinion of the experiment.

A large pockmark—deep enough for Maddock to put both his fists in—marred the stone wall where he had struck it. There were a few large pieces of rock on the floor below but not nearly enough to fill the divot. The rest of it had been pulverized.

"Holy crap," Bones said. "Do that again."

Maddock coughed and tried to blink away some of the grit that now stung his eyes. "I'm not sure I can," he said. "That nearly took my hand off."

"Don't be such a wuss." Bones knelt to retrieve the hatchet. "Here, let the expert take over."

With his free hand, he tugged his T-shirt up and over his head, baring his upper torso. As he wrapped the fabric around the blade he looked over at Rose, and with a mischievous grin, began flexing his pectoral muscles. "Hey, my eyes are up here."

Jade gave a snort of derision.

"I'm not sure that's going to be enough insulation," Maddock warned.

Bones shook his head disparagingly and muttered, "Wuss." Then with the wrapped blade gripped in both hands, he faced the wall. "Better stand back."

"Bones, seriously, maybe you should—"

Bones raised the tomahawk over his head, and then with an impressive rendition of a Cherokee war whoop, brought it down.

Maddock grimaced and looked away, bracing himself in anticipation of another eruption, but even so, the blast caught him flatfooted. There was another flash, as bright as a camera strobe, and then he was engulfed by a cloud of dust and grit, driven by an expanding bubble of uncomfortably warm air—the shockwave of a small detonation.

As some of the dust settled, Maddock spotted

Bones, silhouetted in front of the wall. The big man was protectively hugging both of his hands close to his body, even as he let fly an almost incoherent torrent of invective.

Maddock only caught a few words. "Mother… God… Son of a … Mother." The rest was lost in the din—a grinding sound, like boulders being crushed together, that seemed to be getting louder with each passing second.

"Bones," Jade shouted. "What the hell did you just do?"

Bones fell silent for a moment, then he uncurled one of his arms to point at the wall behind him.

"I did that," Bones said, with more than a trace of pride. "You're welcome."

Through the haze, Maddock could just make out an area that was darker than the surrounding stone. It took him a moment to realize that he was actually looking at nothing—a rectangular void where one of the stone blocks forming the wall had been a moment before. The hole was big enough for even Bones to crawl through.

But the grinding sound was getting louder.

"I think we should—"

Before Maddock could complete his thought, the shape of the neatly defined rectangle of emptiness began to change. The top edge of the hole bowed down, sagging in the middle. Jagged fracture lines began radiating out from the opening like black spiderwebs, and then the entire wall crumbled, unleashing a cascade of rubble that

poured down onto the steps and swept toward them
like an avalanche.

11.

Maddock scrambled back, sidestepping a few larger chunks of debris and ignoring the smaller pieces that brushed against his feet. Bones, closer to the collapse, was knocked backward. He twisted as he fell, throwing his arms wide in a desperate attempt to keep from being swept all the way down. The slide quickly overtook him, partially engulfing him as he slid past Maddock and continued down. Jade, closer to the wall, managed to dance out of the way, but Rose's attempt to dodge the slide took her dangerously close to the edge of the steps.

Fearing that she was about to go over, Maddock threw caution to the wind and, braving the onslaught, charged back up the steps to pull her back. He caught hold of one outflung arm and drew her away from the precipice, but as he did, a large block of stone crashed painfully into his left shin. He pitched forward as his legs were cut out from under him, taking Rose down with him in the fall, and then they were both sliding, caught in the relentless current of crushed stone.

"It's not stopping!"

Jade's shout was barely audible over the ongoing tumult, but Maddock had already realized the truth of her words. The destruction of the stone block had triggered a runaway collapse. Each block that fell out of place dislodged one or two more above it.

The side of the pyramid was collapsing. Worse, the impacts were fracturing the stairwell, obliterating the steps that they would have to ascend in order to reach the surface.

"Keep climbing," he shouted. The admonition was as much for himself as for the others. If they didn't get through that opening quickly, they would be cut off, and in all likelihood, carried down into the depths of the pyramid, entombed forever. "Push through!"

He caught a glimpse of Jade shaking her head, and then she was moving, head ducked low and covered with one upraised arm as she scrambled over the rubble. A moment later, she was gone, vanishing into the dust cloud that still swirled around the opening.

Maddock winced as another rock struck him in the shoulder, but pushed himself up into an awkward kneeling position and crawled forward, putting himself in front of Rose, using his body to shield her. He glanced down the stairs and saw movement in the rockpile. "Bones! You coming?"

A dust-streaked figure emerged from the rubble. "I ain't even breathing heavy, yet."

Maddock just shook his head. Humor—the raunchier the better—was Bones' defensive shield against the universe, but Maddock didn't think it would protect him against the avalanche. He swung his gaze forward again and measured the distance to the now gaping hole in the pyramid's wall.

The damage was spreading out in both

directions, collapsing portions of the wall ahead as well as the one to their immediate right, and as they crumbled, everything above fell inward. The buried pyramid was transforming into a sinkhole.

He leaned close to Rose, shouting to be heard over the din. "Keep moving. Don't stop for anything." Then he started forward, crawling on all fours up the rubble pile. As he neared the top, he could see the opening more distinctly. Jade was crouched just inside, still warding off falling rock with one hand, urging him on with the other. Unfortunately, between him and it was a whole lot of nothing. The last few steps to the opening were gone, fallen into a fissure. It was only about two feet across, but growing wider with each passing second.

Maddock brought his feet up under him in a crouch and then launched himself across the gap. He landed easily, but when Jade reached out with a steadying hand, he did not refuse it. After a moment to catch his balance, he turned and reached out to do the same for Rose.

But in that brief instant, the spot from which he had leaped crumbled away into the fissure, doubling the width of the gap, forcing Rose to retreat.

"Jump!" Jade shouted.

Maddock didn't like Rose's odds of making it across, but seeing no alternatives, he seconded Jade's suggestion and added, "We'll catch you."

Rose's face went slack with trepidation, but she took a deep breath, bent her knees and swung her arms back, gathering momentum for her leap of faith.

Then, seemingly from out of nowhere, Bones appeared beside her. His bare chest and face streaked with dust, he looked more like a giant golem—a creature of living rock—than a man. Without preamble or explanation, he scooped Rose up in his arms, and then propelled her out across the gap.

Maddock caught her easily, pulling her into the relative shelter of the opening. As soon as she was clear, Maddock returned to the edge, "Bones! Jump!"

But Bones was gone.

The woman said nothing; she merely regarded Kismet with a bland, unreadable expression as he climbed into the vehicle, followed by Hauser. Kismet, too, remained silent. One thing he had learned early on in his brief first career as a military intelligence officer was that interrogation was a two-way exchange, with every question, every microexpression, revealing information to the subject.

Yet, even in silence, he knew his reaction had betrayed him.

In truth, he did not think of her as "mother." The circumstances surrounding his birth were shrouded in conjecture and family lore. He was reasonably certain that she was his actual biological parent, but if his suspicions were true, she had served merely as a surrogate—a womb in which he and Ulrich Hauser had gestated. Subsequent events amply demonstrated that she felt no sense of motherly affection or duty toward him. He was simply a variable in some bizarre, secretive experiment. A pawn in the Promethean chess game.

It was true that she had watched over him, shielded him from mortal danger. Hauser had admitted as much in that first encounter. But had she done this because of her feelings for him, or because it advanced her agenda? He suspected the latter.

Even her recent overtures to him, backchanneled through his adoptive father, seemed driven more by her needs—or rather the needs of the traditionalist faction of Prometheus—than by a desire for reconciliation.

The old wisdom about the enemy of his enemy being his friend did not necessarily hold true where Prometheus—or this woman—was concerned. He wasn't yet sure what he wanted her to know about his motives or his loyalties.

Hauser ordered the driver to depart, and as the convoy pulled away, he made a show of adjusting his position, as if trying to get comfortable in preparation for a long trip. After a few seconds of this, he raised his eyes to the woman. "Mother, look who turned up." A glance to Kismet, then back to the woman. "Wait, have you two actually met?" He laughed. "It's funny, Nick. I got to have her as a mother, but you got to keep her name. I'm not sure which one of us got the better end of that deal."

Kismet once more fought a losing battle to hide his reaction. His unusual surname was one more piece of family lore he had largely taken for granted. Now, at least, he had one answer.

The woman flashed an irritated look at Hauser, but said nothing.

"Mother," Hauser went on. "I brought Nick here in the hopes that he could convince you to tell me how to find Olympus."

She stared at Hauser a moment longer, her eyes narrowing contemptuously. Then she turned to Kismet. "I know what he wants," she said. "What do you want?"

He weighed all his possible answers. Did hedare tell her the truth? Reveal that the lives of Maddock and the others hung in the balance? Would she understand that he was just biding his time, waiting for an opportunity to turn the tables on Hauser? Would she believe that the last thing he wanted was for his psychotic twin brother to gain possession of the elemental artifacts and all the other secrets in the Prometheus vault?

He decided to answer with a different truth. "I want answers."

The corners of her mouth twitched and began to curl upward. "So, my boys are finally getting along. It's about damn time."

"Bones!"

Maddock leaned out of the tunnel opening, searching the dust-shrouded steps for any sign of his friend, but as he did, he felt the edge of the opening giving way beneath him. He scrambled back a fraction of a second ahead of the collapse. The passage filled with dust. The tumult reached a deafening climax, the floor under him shaking in a sustained tremor.

And then all was still.

Maddock crawled forward into the settling dust cloud until he reached the edge. "Bones!"

He waved his hand, trying to swat the cloud away. Somehow, he had managed to hang onto his phone and now shone its light into the emptiness beyond. The motes swirled away, affected more by gravity than anything he was doing, but after a few seconds, it cleared enough for him to see what lay beyond.

There wasn't enough left of the hollow pyramid to recognize what it had once been. The stone blocks that had formed its walls and the long descending staircase now lay mostly in a jumble on the floor of an enormous cavern—or rather a sinkhole. Without the pyramid to support it, the roof had collapsed in. Looking up, Maddock could see starlight.

Movement from below caught his eye, drawing his attention back to the ruin of the cavern. A hand had appeared from just beyond the edge of the passage opening, fingers splayed out, trying to find purchase on the rough surface.

"Bones!" Maddock cried again, his earlier desperation washed away with a flood of relief. Though he couldn't fathom how Bones had managed to accomplish it, the big man had evidently leaped across the spreading fissure and onto the exposed cavern wall where he had clung to the bare rock, riding out the violent collapse of the pyramid.

Maddock gripped his friend's wrist in both hands and leaned back, giving the big man an assist. Bones' other hand came up and then with a dynamic heave, his upper torso rose into view, allowing him to wriggle forward onto the floor of the passage where he collapsed and lay motionless for several seconds. But despite his obvious exhaustion, behind his mask of dust and grime, Bones was grinning.

"Well," he said, "I think that finally settles the question of who's the best climber."

Maddock gaped at him in disbelief. "Seriously?" He shook his head. "Don't you mean luckiest?"

"Aw, you're just jealous, 'cause you couldn't have solved that problem."

"Bones, you *caused* the problem."

"You know, that's always been your problem. You see a silver lining and you start looking for the dark cloud. We made it out of there." He straightened, evidently remembering something.

"Oh, speaking of silver linings…"

He reached to his back pocket and produced the hatchet head. The metal gleamed brightly, without a single scratch to mar its surface. He handed it to Rose. "I think this belongs to you."

"And speaking of dark clouds," Jade put in, "What are we going to do now?"

"Do?" asked Bones. "You mean aside from crawling out of this hell hole and heading back to the hotel for beer, a shower and a bed?"

"We have to help Nick."

"Help him?" Bones snorted. "After what he did? Not a chance."

"Bones, even you can't be that thick. He did that to save us."

"If you call leaving us buried alive 'saving us'?"

Maddock jumped in. "She's right. And there's an even better reason to go after them. We need to stop Hauser from getting his hands on that fourth relic."

"How are we supposed to do that? We don't have a clue where it is."

Maddock considered this question for a moment. "I think I know someone who might be able to help with that."

12.

Long Island, New York

Professor accelerated, shooting straight across three lanes of oncoming traffic, before hooking left and joining the flow of traffic heading the other direction. The car fishtailed back and forth, confounding his efforts to regain control.

"Look out," Jimmy warned, pointing a finger at a gray van directly ahead and coming up fast.

Professor swerved over into the inside lane, almost sideswiping the van, and then they were past.

Ahead, the red sports car he was pursuing took a hard-right turn.

"Turn right," Jimmy cried. "Stay with him!"

"I know," Professor snapped, and then muttered under his breath. "This is impossible."

He steered hard, realizing only as the front end swung around that the turn wasn't merely a hard right—it was a hairpin, curving almost completely around to ascend up the hillside that ran parallel to the highway. Even so, Professor mistimed the turn. The front end bounced up onto the sidewalk, narrowly missing a group of people who were standing on the corner, evidently waiting for a bus. Suddenly, the hillside was right in front of him. He tried to simultaneously brake and cut to the right, but failed to do either one. The car slammed into the hill, ejecting him into the air like a rag doll, tumbling in slow motion.

The wall-mounted 120-inch plasma screen went gray, the image frozen, and then a single word appeared slashed across its middle. "Wasted."

Jimmy sat back laughing. "Oh, dude. That was epic."

Professor resisted the urge to hurl the wireless computer-game controller against the wall. "I don't know why I let you talk me into this."

"Right, because there are so many other things we could be doing right now," Jimmy countered, still chuckling.

Professor sighed resignedly and settled back to wait for his character to respawn. Jimmy wasn't wrong. With the Prometheus situation still unresolved, Jimmy didn't dare venture out into the world, much less return to his life, and until Tam Broderick said otherwise, babysitting Jimmy was his top priority, which meant he wasn't going anywhere either.

There were far worse places to spend a week. Christian Garral's home was, by most definitions, a mansion, which meant there was plenty to keep them occupied. Garral himself was both hospitable and garrulous, which meant plenty of good food and drink, and even better conversation. Still, after a few days, Professor felt he had exhausted the list of intellectual diversions, which was why he had decided to join Jimmy in the game room. The journalist had hardly left the room during the course of their stay. Evidently, Garral's Alienware computer provided a transcendent gaming experience. For his part, Professor was astonished at the cinematic quality of the games, many of which had storylines as complex as some novels, with gameplay that required lightning reflexes and eye-hand coordination. After a few hours of watching as a spectator, Jimmy had offered him a turn.

It had been a long time since he had felt so completely inept. Learning to use the controls was like learning how to type in a foreign language or play an unfamiliar musical instrument. The in-game tutorial had helped. A little. But now he was on his own and failing spectacularly at tasks that, in real life, he could have accomplished with ease. The worst part was, he felt compelled to keep playing.

A gentle knock on the game room door distracted him. He looked up to see Garral enter the room, phone in hand. "Excuse the interruption gentleman, but I think you'll want to join me for this call."

He placed the phone on the coffee table in front of the couch where Professor and Jimmy sat. "You're on speaker, Mr. Maddock."

"Dane?" Jimmy sat up. So did Professor.

There was a brief lag and then Maddock's voice issued from the device. "Hey, Jimmy. Professor, you're there, too?"

"I am, Dane."

"Great. I think we're going to need all hands on deck for this one." Maddock then launched into a narrative describing everything that had happened subsequent to their discovery of the plane wreck.

Professor was astonished to learn that Jade and Kismet had gotten embroiled in the adventure. While he had been babysitting Jimmy, they, along with Dane and Bones, had traveled to the literal ends of the earth, facing danger and making incredible discoveries. He was also surprisingly relieved to hear that Jade had come through it all without serious injury. Looking out for her was, after all, still his primary responsibility.

But as Maddock related the events that had just transpired in Egypt, he realized that Jade's continued safety was far from guaranteed. Prometheus—or rather, Ulrich Hauser, the apparent leader of the radical faction—was close to unlocking some kind of supernatural power that would fundamentally change the shape of the world, and Jade, along with Maddock and Bones, were intent on stopping them.

Even if it cost them their lives.

"We know that Hauser is going after the fourth elemental relic," Maddock concluded, "And it sounds like Prometheus has it. We've got to beat him to it. Unfortunately, we don't have a clue about its location."

Garral's already grave frown deepened. "I'm sorry, but I don't have that information. The location of the vault is a secret known only by a handful of Prometheus' leaders. And their identities are secret as well."

"You know someone though," Professor put in. "You've got an inside source."

Garral nodded slowly, clearly conflicted at the position he had been put in. "Yes. If anyone would know, she would. And since this concerns Nick, I believe she will help."

"She?" asked Maddock. "You're talking about Nick's mom, aren't you?"

Garral's chagrined look was answer enough. "Unfortunately, making contact with her is equally problematic. She's always been the one to initiate our conversations."

"How do you usually communicate?" asked Jimmy.

"Mostly burner phones, delivered by couriers. Sometimes SMS chat, but she always uses a throwaway account."

Jimmy's eyes narrowed in concentration. "If you'd be willing to let me poke around in your files, I might be able to get a line on her."

Garral nodded. Jimmy immediately picked up the wireless keyboard, closed out the video game, and went to work.

"That sounds like it's going to take some time," intoned Maddock. "And we don't have a lot of that to spare right now. Hauser's already on the move."

"I can definitely help with that," Jimmy replied. "He'll probably fly out. Private jet or chartered flight, right? He'll have to file a flight plan."

"I'm sure he'll cover his tracks," Professor countered.

"I'm sure he will, too. But I've got mad skills." Jimmy entered a few keystrokes, and a new window opened on the plasma screen. Under a blue header which bore the logo of the International Civil Aviation Organization, a table displayed all the flights departing Alexandria, Egypt.

"He also doesn't know that we made it out of that tomb," Maddock added. "He might not be as careful as he ordinarily would. My guess is, he's got just one thing on his mind. He'll probably go straight to wherever it is he's going."

Jimmy just nodded absently and continued navigating the site, changing back and forth between screens faster than Professor could follow, and after a few seconds he stopped trying. "Dane, you should probably head for Cairo immediately. From there, you'll have a lot more travel options, and hopefully by the time you get there, we'll have a better idea of where they're headed."

"Beat you to it," Jimmy announced before Maddock could reply. "I know where they're going."

Professor glanced up at the screen and saw displayed the information for a charter flight that was scheduled to depart Alexandria in a matter of minutes. He blinked. "How do you know it's that one?"

"Well, for starters, the flight plan was just amended thirty minutes ago. The original destination was Paris, but now there's an addendum. Longyearben, Norway. My backtrace on the hacker that locked me out of my proxy network ended at the SvalSat facility just outside Longyearben. At the time, I thought they had outsmarted me. Roped me down a rabbit hole, but I think maybe I outsmarted myself."

Maddock's voice sounded after the requisite delay. "But that could just be a coincidence, right? We can't afford to run down that rabbit hole after you."

"Sure, it's possible. But Longyearben is remote. It's not the kind of place you just decide to visit on a whim."

A new and familiar voice issued from the speaker—"Bones" Bonebrake. "When you say 'remote'…?"

"Longyearben is in the Svalbard Archipelago," Professor supplied. "It's north of the Arctic Circle, the closest city to the North Pole."

"Svalbard," Maddock said. "Isn't that where the Doomsday Vault is?"

"The technical name for it is the Svalbard Global Seed Vault, but yes, it's a man-made cave carved into a mountain, containing frozen samples of diverse flora, against the possibility of a catastrophic event."

"You're shitting me," Bones said with a groan. "Another frozen wasteland? Why can't they ever put these things somewhere nice? Like Maui?"

"The surrounding permafrost helps keep the vault at a constant temperature of zero degrees Fahrenheit." He paused a beat, then added. "The Seed Vault would be the perfect cover for a

Prometheus treasure vault. I think Jimmy's right. That's where they're going."

"Then that's where we have to go," Maddock said. "Mr. Garral, I hate to ask but—"

Garral cut him off. "You don't need to. There will be a jet waiting for you in Cairo. And I'll be waiting for you in Oslo."

"We all will," Professor said. He glanced at Garral and got a nod of confirmation.

After ending the call, Garral gave a heavy sigh. "People talk about being willing to go to the ends of the earth for their children. It seems I'll be doing that quite literally."

Professor had no doubt that Garral was capable of enduring whatever hardships lay ahead, and Kismet was his son, after all.

Jimmy cleared his throat. "Umm, I need some clarification on something. When you said we would all be there—?"

"I meant all of us. You heard Dane. All hands on deck."

"I think I'd be a lot more use to everyone if I stayed right here."

Professor fixed Jimmy with a hard stare. "The Svalbard Seed Vault is one of the most secure facilities on earth. If anyone can beat their security system, it's you."

"I can walk you through remotely—"

Professor shook his head. "That's not going to cut it. We'll need your expertise on the ground."

Jimmy blanched.

"This shouldn't be hard for you," Professor went on. "I've seen you in action. You walked into the NSA, for God's sake. Just think of it as a real-life video game."

"A video game where I could get killed."

Professor gripped the other man's shoulder. "Jimmy, do you remember ringing the bell?"

For a moment, Jimmy appeared confused by the non-sequitur, but then his expression tightened and he jerked away from Professor. "How dare you—"

"For a long time, I thought of you as just another quitter. Big dreams and a little heart. But I was wrong about you. You just had a bad day."

Jimmy glowered at him for several seconds, then spoke through clenched teeth. "You gotta point, coach?"

"You promised Dane that you and he would finish BUD/S together. You remember that?"

"I've done more for Maddock than you can possibly imagine."

"This isn't about Maddock. It's about you. Finishing what you started. Proving it to yourself."

Jimmy's eyes danced. He glanced over at Garral, who looked on in stony silence, and then back to Professor. "You can't make me go, you know."

"Actually, I could." He paused a beat, letting that sink in, then added. "But I'm not going to because you're not going to ring the bell this time."

He didn't give Jimmy a chance to respond but turned to Garral.

"We'd better get moving."

PART THREE: HEAVEN KNOWS

13.

From a distance, the Svalbard Global Seed Vault resembled nothing less than a charcoal gray shark fin, inexplicably tipped with an enormous glittering diamond, knifing through an endless sapphire sea. The sea of course was frozen, a white snowscape that so perfectly reflected the night sky—at this time of year and so far north, there was only night sky— it was impossible to tell where one began and the other ended.

The diamond was an illuminated art piece entitled *Perpetual Repercussion*, a flat pane of glass behind which mirrors and prisms redirected and amplified natural light when available, and artificial light, delivered by fiber optic cables, during the long winter to give the piece its glow. It now shone like a beacon guiding the riders on their snowmobiles to the vault's doorstep.

Kismet drove his snowmobile—a SkiDoo MXZ 800 rented from an adventure tour outfitter in Longyearbyen—with one of Hauser's men seated directly behind him in the one-up position. The passenger was armed, the driver was not. Hauser's trust only went so far, it seemed. Two more SkiDoos carried four more of Hauser's security team. Hauser drove the fourth, with their mother seated behind him.

"I don't even know what to call you," Kismet had told the woman, the previous night during the drive to the airport in Alexandria, even before she had revealed the location of Olympus.

"I don't suppose I could convince you to call me 'mom,'" she had said with a wry smile. When he didn't respond, she went on. "Call me Leda."

"Leda," Kismet echoed. In Greek mythology, Leda had been the mortal mother of Castor and Pollux—twins sired by different fathers, one mortal—Tyndareus, king of Sparta—and one immortal—Zeus, king of the gods. Kismet doubted it was her real name, but chose not to press the issue.

"I'm sure you must be full of questions," she said. "I've wanted to answer them for so long."

"Why didn't you?"

He had an idea what her answer would be. During their second encounter, Hauser had told him about Prometheus' grand experiment, the two of them, products of some kind of engineered union, separated at birth, one—Kismet—sent out into the world with no knowledge of his heritage, watched over and occasionally protected by Prometheus, but never told the truth.

She smiled ruefully. "It wasn't the right time."

"And now it is?"

"Now it is."

When they were in the air aboard Hauser's chartered jet, winging north to a planned refueling stop in Paris before heading on to Longyearbyen, she told the story from the beginning over a bottle of Bordeaux. Hauser shared the bottle with her, saying nothing. Kismet declined.

"Much of what I am about to tell you is conjecture," Leda began, "but it is, we believe, an accurate approximation of the true prehistory of our world.

"There are common threads woven through the various mythologies of creation. One of these is a story of gods or god-like beings, putting on corporeal bodies, walking among men, taking mortal women for mates. In most stories, the offspring of the union is a demi-god—Gilgamesh, Perseus, Herakles. There are demigods in Hindu mythology. Norse. Celtic… As I said, it is a constant thread. In the religions of the Abrahamic tradition, they are called Nephilim—the mighty ones, and are said to be the children of fallen angels." Leda paused to take a sip of wine and perhaps also let the gravity of her story sink in.

"These stories are all true," she said, and then quickly amended. "After a fashion."

"Let me guess. You don't want to say it's aliens, but…"

Leda did not smile. "We call them 'the Ancients.' Rather prosaic, I suppose, but it suffices. We do not speculate on their origins, but we do believe that they were non-corporeal entities. They constructed artificial organic bodies to use as vessels—"

"Artificial organic? That sounds like an oxymoron."

"Artificial because they were created," Leda clarified. "The product of artifice. Organic because they were made to perfectly simulate the organic functions of a human body, right down to procreation.

"What happened after that is not known with certainty. Some believe the Flood myths—another nearly universal thread—are evidence of some kind of upheaval that prompted their departure, as described in early Jewish and Christian documents. Others think they simply grew tired of their existence here and moved on. Returned whence they came. Whatever the explanation, they left those magnificent bodies behind. We know this because we have several of them at Olympus."

Despite the lead-in, the revelation caught Kismet off guard. "You have the... The god-bodies?"

"God-bodies," Hauser said with a chuckle. "I like that."

Leda smiled. "They appear as statues of gold, and indeed, many were discovered in temple ruins. The gold exhibits an unusual chemical signature—a stable anion that can store electrical current."

"Like the Golden Fleece," Kismet murmured.

Leda gave a satisfied nod. "You hear the truth of it, I can tell." She paused, took another sip. "You may recall in the legend that Jason encountered a metal giant named Talos. In some versions, he is a god, in others, an automaton created by Hephaestus. Regardless, Jason defeated him by removing a nail from Talos' heel, which allowed his blood—a molten substance called *ichor*, the blood of the gods—to drain out.

"About fifty years ago, Prometheus scientists made careful examinations of the god-bodies and discovered traces of a liquid metal that reacted to a strong electrical current. And when these traces were reintroduced into the god-bodies, they began to show signs of activity.

"Not life," she added quickly. "Something more akin to neuro-muscular activity. Like a postmortem muscle spasm. It is possible that ancient priests with a rudimentary understanding of electricity might have elicited a similar response, seemingly animating the statues of their gods. In any event, the effect was short-lived and the sample of charged *ichor* evaporated, but it was enough to inform our theory of the Ancients. And to begin designing other experiments."

Kismet suddenly felt nauseated, his head spinning with vertigo that had nothing to do with motion sickness from the flight. "Experiments," he rasped.

It wasn't a question. He already knew the answer.

The party dismounted their snowmobiles in front of a wide metal ramp that rose to the double doors at the entrance. From this perspective, the entrance to the seed vault looked like an ominous rectangular monolith—three stories high. The doors occupied the lower third of the towering edifice. A louvered ventilation screen, part of the refrigeration system, filled the middle, and the top was dominated by the glittering illuminated *Perpetual Repercussion.*

The entrance to the seed vault was only a short ride by snowmobile, though it seemed to take much longer. The desolate landscape had a haunted aura about it, which their arrival did not dispel.

Kismet glanced up at the video camera mounted above the door. There was no permanent staff at the Global Seed Vault—it was a repository, not a research facility. The only reason for anyone to visit, aside from occasional maintenance, was to add to the collection of seeds.

It was, Kismet thought, the perfect cover for the Prometheus operation—a repository of a different sort.

Leda had briefly explained that there was an "arrangement" between the Norwegian government and Prometheus, which was why their unscheduled visit would raise no alarms.

She advanced to the doors, producing the ring of keys she had retrieved from a vacant guest apartment in Longyearbyen. Kismet surmised the dwelling was intended to provide temporary housing for visiting members of Prometheus' inner circle. In the sparsely populated city, where turnover was high, what was one more empty apartment?

Kismet recalled reading that no one person had all the keys and access codes necessary to enter the vault. Evidently, the "arrangement" included an exception for the senior leadership of Prometheus.

Leda used three different keys to open deadbolt locks and then pulled the door open. Hauser pushed past her, though in fact there was little to see beyond the doors. The entrance was unremarkable; a long corridor of unpainted concrete illuminated by hanging fluorescent lights. Though shielded somewhat from the elements, there was no relief from the bitter Arctic chill, so the party remained bundled up against the cold. Enveloped in heavy parkas, faces hidden behind neoprene masks, the only way for Kismet to differentiate the members of the group was by seeing who was armed and who was not. His mother and he were the only ones in the latter category. That commonality however did not make them allies.

Leda had not given Kismet time to process the revelation. "When it became apparent that two viable embryos had been cultivated, the decision was made to separate the two of you. In the old stories, demigods who were unaware of their parentage were often noble, heroic, while those who grew up knowing the truth were cruel and oppressive. Entitled."

She glanced sidelong at Hauser who laughed loudly. "And why not?" he said, deflecting the implicit criticism. "They were superior."

Leda ignored the comment. "In every experiment, there is a control. We found a suitable father to raise you, give you a good life... A full life. Every choice that you made was yours and yours alone."

Kismet drew in a deep breath. "The mission in Iraq. Was that a mistake?"

Leda and Hauser shared a look, an unspoken conversation, then she answered. "In a word, yes. The defector was a recent initiate into Prometheus. He knew of you, knew just enough to believe that you would be able to give him and his family safe passage out of Iraq."

"So why didn't you let me?" Kismet turned his stare on Hauser. "Why did you have to kill his whole family?"

Hauser merely shrugged, but Leda was not so dismissive. "There was a disagreement about how to proceed. You know how that argument ended. The consequences of that decision nearly destroyed us. It was the genesis of the schism that still divides us. More importantly however, it set you on the path to discovery. Every demigod must one day awaken to his true nature. The time for experimentation is over. It's time for you to embrace who and what you are." She glanced at Hauser again. "Both of you."

Kismet shook his head. The revelations had left him numb. Hollowed out. *This can't be true. Ancient alien visitors. Demigods. This is just another one of their head games.*

Yet, he knew it was true. Every word of it.

He straightened, took a deep breath. "I thought you two were at each other's throats. You're with the traditionalists. He's leading the radicals. Now we're all one big happy family?"

"He's right, you know," Hauser said, answering quickly as if the question had been weighing on him. "This is so like you, mother. Manipulative and duplicitous. I'm sorry, but I don't trust you."

She shook her head. "You were always a foolish boy, Rick. Headstrong. Refusing to wait your turn. This was always going to be your destiny."

Hauser's eyes narrowed. "You're lying. You opposed me at every turn."

"Because it wasn't time," Leda hissed.

"I decide when it's time."

"No," she said, flatly. "I made that decision when I told you where to find Olympus."

Hauser regarded her for several seconds, then

without looking away, addressed Kismet. "What do you think, brother? Sending us to the end of the earth like this... Is she telling the truth, or leading us into a trap?" He shrugged. "I can handle whatever she throws at me, but the clock is ticking for your friends."

For the first time since their introduction, a look of alarm came over Leda's features. She had not been aware of the leverage Hauser had used to convince Kismet to join him. She stared at Kismet, brows furrowing in apprehension, but just as quickly, relaxed again.

"Whatever else I am," she said, "I am your mother. You have a destiny. Both of you. And I want you to succeed. Prometheus was only ever the means to that end. Olympus holds the key to your ascendance... Your apotheosis. You will become gods among men, and I... Well, I will be the mother of gods."

That, Kismet believed.

There was another double door at the end of the corridor, this one secured with an electronic lock. Leda tapped the access code into the keypad and the lock disengaged. Beyond it lay a long descending tunnel with curved sides covered in ice. As soon as they were through the doors, Leda pulled them shut again, locking them inside.

Despite his polar garments, Kismet felt colder

here, as if the dry air was sucking the life out of him. They were deep inside the mountain now, surrounded by permafrost, though in reality the temperature in the vault was artificially maintained by refrigeration units. The electricity that powered the so-called Doomsday Vault was supplied by Norway's only coal-fired power plant, located in Longyearbyen.

They passed by a few unmarked doors, coming to a T-junction. The ice accumulation here was even thicker, a couple inches at least, glittering white in contrast to the gray concrete floor. Leda steered them to the right, down a short hall that dead-ended. On the left, almost completely hidden by the ice scrim was another set of double doors.

Leda brushed the ice away from the door level with one gloved hand, and then slotted in a key from her ring. The door opened, revealing a small room with another set of doors against the far wall. When they were all inside the room, she pulled the door shut, sealing them in. Kismet could feel a subtle change in both temperature and air pressure. This was an airlock, though not a hermetically sealed one. With the outer door closed, the electronic lock on the inner door released automatically. Beyond was a room that looked like an enormous warehouse, with long rows of metal rack shelving, but every single one completely empty.

Hauser swore angrily. "There's nothing here, mother."

"As far as the public is concerned," Leda explained patiently, "there are three vaults here. Currently, only vault two is in use and it is not yet at full capacity. There is, however, another vault of which the public has no knowledge."

She advanced to the open cage gate and started down the middle row. Curious despite himself, Kismet hurried after her, with Hauser and his men trailing behind.

Even up close, the back wall appeared to be covered in ice like everything else, but as she approached a spot near the corner, Leda stripped off her right glove and reached out to touch the white crystals bare-handed. A chunk of ice the size of a dinner plate separated from the wall, swinging away on hidden hinges to reveal a square of black glass. She pressed her hand flat against it, and after a few seconds, a light flashed behind the glass. A biometric palm reader, Kismet realized.

As soon as Leda removed her hand from the glass, a loud hiss echoed in the still air, and then the entire wall began to move, separating into halves which swiveled inward to create a passage into another vault, considerably larger than the space they currently occupied. In fact, Kismet could not see to the far end. There were no racks of shelves here, but the vault was by no means empty. Arrayed on the bare floor, lined up like gigantic chess pieces awaiting the beginning of a game, were dozens of sculpted human figures, each one at least eight feet in height—some much larger than that—and each one gleaming brightly with light reflecting from their polished golden skin.

Leda calmly replaced her glove. When the walls stopped moving, she gestured forward. "Well boys, would you like to meet your father?"

Not really, Kismet thought sourly, but before he could voice his revulsion at the idea, Hauser spoke up.

"Sorry mother, but the family reunion will have to wait." He held up the backpack he'd taken from Rose in Alexandria, but there was something unusual about it now. The straps were pulled taut, but instead of dangling straight down, gravity tugging the contents toward the center of the earth, the bag was hanging sideways. The elemental relics inside were being drawn toward something inside the vault. Hauser grinned hungrily. "I have more pressing business."

14.

Dane Maddock peered through the lenses of his Nikon Aculon A211 binoculars and studied the area around the dark wedge protruding from the mountainside below. The surrounding snow was glowing a brighter shade of blue in the reflected light of the illuminated art piece, and he was easily able to distinguish four snowmobiles parked nearby. They had arrived just a few minutes earlier, the riders dismounting and heading into that imposing structure with the ominous nickname—the Doomsday Vault. Maddock kept scanning the area, ensuring that none of the recently arrived party was remaining outside to guard the snowmobiles. When he was satisfied that this was the case, he lowered the binoculars and unclipped a Motorola T600 Talkabout radio from the tactical gear vest he wore over his North Face parka. He keyed the mic and spoke. "Bones, you copy?"

"Only when I don't know the answer," came the reply.

Maddock rolled his eyes. It was a terrible joke, but at least Bones had stopped griping about the cold. "I think this is the place," Maddock continued. "Those snowmobiles that passed us went straight to the seed vault and stopped. Four machines, eight riders."

There was a momentary pause, probably just

long enough for Bones to relay the information to the rest of the group, and then he spoke again. "You sure they aren't just there to shovel the walk?"

"Pretty sure," Maddock said.

Christian Garral had been unable to reach his contact inside Prometheus, which meant there had been no way to confirm the supposition that the secret facility was located at or near the Global Seed Vault, but given the timing, there was little doubt as to the real identity of the group that had just entered it.

There had been another plane parked on the runway of the Svalbard Longyear airport, and a check of the tail numbers confirmed it was the same plane that had left Alexandria almost twelve hours earlier. A discreet inquiry revealed that the first plane had landed a little over an hour before them—two arrivals in such a short time span was a noteworthy event on the remote island—and while they had not been able to confirm the identity of the passengers, they at least knew how many of them had deplaned. Seven men and one woman.

That news had plainly startled Christian Garral. The woman, he told them, was in all likelihood his contact inside Prometheus—Leda Hauser nee Kismet. Nick Kismet's mother.

During the flight to Oslo, Maddock and Bones had teleconferenced with Professor, and done extensive map reconnaissance of Spitzbergen Island, where the Seed Vault was situated. The vault was only about half-a-mile from the airport, so rather than traveling into Longyearbyen to rent snowmobiles, the decision was made to depart directly from the plane, traveling overland on foot using snowshoes. Bones had grumbled about the cold until Professor pointed out that the exertion of hiking through the snow would generate so much body heat that freezing to death would be the least of his concerns. After that, Bones had complained about overheating.

A half-mile snowshoe trek would be no picnic, so Maddock had given everyone the option of remaining behind at the plane. He wasn't actually that worried about their physical ability; Rose and Jade were certainly capable. Garral had been a professional mountaineer and explorer in his younger days, and still appeared to be in prime condition. Maddock's real concern was what would happen when they finally confronted Hauser. He saw no outcome that did not end in violence, and in such a situation, he would need people trained for combat like himself—Bones and Professor had that training. Everyone else would be a liability.

On the other hand, a few extra guns might make all the difference, and while the others weren't former SEALs, they all had some experience. In any event, no one had taken him up on the offer, though Jimmy had shifted nervously in his seat, shooting glances at Professor. Maddock had no idea what the latter had said to convince Jimmy to tag along, and Jimmy wasn't talking.

Maybe later, when this was over, he'd have to

ply Jimmy with some Wild Turkey.

Jimmy, Professor, and Garral had been waiting for them in Oslo, along with snowshoes, cold weather gear, and even weapons—hunting rifles, which Garral explained were necessary for travel to the Svalbard territory where polar bears outnumbered people. Garral had also discreetly supplied Maddock and Bones each with a not-strictly-legal Glock 20 10-millimeter semi-automatic pistol.

While Bones and Professor led the main party up a poorly marked road from the airport, Maddock scouted ahead. His intention was to climb partway up the side of the mountain into which the seed vault had been carved in order to get a top-down look at the site, but shortly after beginning his ascent, he'd heard the noise of snowmobiles coming down the road from Longyearbyen.

The riders had blazed past, taking no note of his tracks, and continued on to the Seed Vault.

Hauser had won the race to reach the secret Prometheus facility, but not by much.

Maddock keyed his radio mic again. "Come on up. I'll meet you at the entrance."

Bones said something—it might have been something off-color or simply an acknowledgment, but Maddock had already returned the walkie-talkie to his vest and brought his rifle—a Remington 700, bolt action with a wooden stock—to the low ready. He started down the hill, backtracking down to the road below. Polar bears were a real concern, but avalanche was an even greater danger, especially here on the side of a mountain, so he moved slowly, careful to avoid triggering a slide.

As he neared the road, he spotted a line of human figures trudging toward him from the east. They were still a good hundred yards away, moving slower than his average walking pace, hampered somewhat by fatigue and unfamiliarity with snowshoes, but they were moving. Rather than wait for them, he turned toward their destination and continued to the entrance to the seed vault, moving easily in the trail of packed snow left by the snowmobiles.

Maddock stopped at the metal walkway and unclipped his bindings and stepped out of his snowshoes, stabbing the paddle-shaped aluminum frames into a snowbank, tail-end down. He glanced back and saw the rest of his party approaching. The towering figure in the lead—almost certainly Bones—was advancing at a jog, his rifle at the ready, but the rest were spaced out unevenly behind him, with some clearly struggling to stay on their feet, using their ski poles for balance.

"Come on," he muttered, knowing that his exhortation would go unheard. "We're running out of time."

He couldn't wait any longer. As soon as Bones reached him, he gestured to the door. "Cover me. I'm going to try the door."

Bones nodded and, without pausing to remove his snowshoes, took a knee and aimed his rifle at the door. Maddock let his rifle hang from its sling and reached inside his parka for the Glock pistol. Extreme cold could play havoc with semi-automatic weapons, freezing ordinary gun lubricants and deforming plastic and metal components, so he had kept the weapon inside the coat, close to his body to minimize exposure to the sub-zero temperatures, even though doing so meant that it wouldn't be within easy reach. He held the pistol in his extended right hand, and reached for the door handle with his left.

A nasally voice cried out. "Wait!"

Maddock grimaced, and turned back to see one of the figures—it had to be Jimmy—stumbling forward, waving his arms. He made it a few steps before the front of his snowshoe snagged the snow and his attempt to run ended with him going face down, half-buried in white powder. He struggled back up and started forward again.

As impressed as he was at his friend's tenacity, Maddock shook his head. "Jimmy, we have to go in. Now. Get behind some cover."

Jimmy kept advancing coming up right behind Bones. To his credit, he made it the rest of the way without falling. "Just wait," he said again, panting to catch his breath. "Wait. I didn't let you guys drag me all the way out here so I could just sit in the rear with the gear."

Maddock wasn't sure what Jimmy was trying to say. Did he want to be part of the assault?

Jimmy wasn't reaching for his gun however.

Instead, he unslung his backpack and pulled out a laptop computer. He tromped across the bridge to join Maddock in the lee of the entrance, and knelt beside him, balancing the computer on one knee.

"Jimmy, I don't think you're going to get WiFi out here," Bones said. He still had his rifle up, ready to fire at anyone who might come through the door.

"And that's why you don't get paid to think," Jimmy shot back without looking up. As the screen lit up, he stripped off his gloves and began tapping at the keyboard. After a few seconds of this, he let out a whoop of triumph. "Yes!" He pumped his fist, but then thrust the bare hand into the depths of his parka for warmth. "As I suspected, the security system here transmits data by secure satellite connection."

Understanding dawned for Maddock. "So you can hack into it?"

"I can hack into it," Jimmy confirmed, resuming his keystrokes. "It's a secure transmission, like a sat-phone. Give me a minute."

Maddock pursed his lips. Even a minute seemed like an indulgence. And even if Jimmy succeeded, it wouldn't change the fact that they would, in all likelihood, have to fight their way in. "Just keep at it," he told Jimmy. He glanced back and saw that the rest of the group had arrived. "Professor. Come back me up. We'll go in—"

"Got it!" Jimmy announced. He turned the laptop so Maddock could see the screen, which was divided into several smaller screens displaying what appeared to be nondescript hallways and empty warehouses.

"This is real time?"

"Live from the Doomsday Vault," Jimmy confirmed. He pointed to the screen, his finger moving from one static image to the next. "This is the entrance. These are different angles of the tunnel. These cover the vault doors. And here's vault two, the only one currently in use."

The indicated image showed what looked like the aisles of a big box store, but instead of bulk groceries, the rack shelves held gray tote boxes.

"Not much to look at," Jimmy said, almost apologetically.

"There's no one there."

Jimmy just shrugged. "Sorry. Maybe they're standing somewhere the cameras can't see."

Maddock shook off his disappointment. "Good work, Jimmy. At least we know what's on the other side of this door." He reached out for it again and tugged on the handle.

The door swung open. Unlocked.

Leading with his pistol, Maddock moved inside, but the interior was empty, just as the video feed had indicated. At the far end of a short hallway was another door with a numeric keypad mounted on the wall beside it. He hurried forward and tried the door handle.

Locked.

He looked at the keypad then back at the open door behind him. The others were already filing in.

"Jimmy, can you open this?"

The other man started to shake his head, but then stopped and came forward to take a closer look at it. "Maybe."

He said it slowly, pausing between the syllables so that it sounded like two separate words. "May. Be." Maddock took that as a good sign.

Jimmy dipped into his pack and brought out a black cable with plugs on either end. He inserted one into his laptop and then found a port on the underside of the keypad into which he plugged the other end.

Maddock took a step back, letting the other man do his magic. Then he felt a tugging on his arm. It was Rose. "Dane, look."

She was holding a piece of parachute cord, from which dangled the adamantine-infused tomahawk head. But it wasn't hanging down. Instead, it was pulling straight ahead, pointing right at the door.

"Definitely the right place," she said with a grin of triumph.

15.

The fourth elemental relic was not a tablet upon which the secrets of alchemy had been inscribed, nor was it a sword in the conventional sense, but it was a large green crystal, shining with a brilliant glow that seemed too bright to merely be a reflection of the overhead fluorescent bulbs. Kismet could see how it might easily be described as a sword. The crystal was flat and broad—about four inches across—and long, at least twenty-four inches, tapering to points at either end.

One other detail made it appear sword-like. It was held in a two-handed grip over the chest of a figure lying in repose on a bier near the center of the vault, a remarkably life-like image of an athletic looking man. Like the giant statues they had passed on the way in, it appeared to be made entirely of gold.

There was a strange energy radiating from the golden figure—not the light from the emerald, but something else. Something invisible, a hum of potential energy. The crystal itself seemed to be vibrating imperceptibly, straining against the fixed grip, no doubt attracted to the elemental relics Hauser carried in the backpack. The hum was either above or below the threshold of human hearing, but Kismet felt it in every cell of his body—a vague but growing sense of unease. He swallowed, his mouth dry.

"Alexander the Great," Leda explained, though Kismet had already guessed as much.

"Was he one of your Ancients?" he asked.

"No. Just a man who thought he was a demi-god. When he died, his body was placed in a golden coffin cast from his form. According to some historical accounts, the golden coffin was replaced by one made of glass by Ptolemy X, so the gold could be melted down in order to pay debts incurred in his war to hold the throne he'd taken from his older brother. The act so outraged the citizens of Alexandria that he was deposed, exiled and eventually killed. In actuality, the priests of Hermes arranged a deception. They gave Ptolemy gold out of their own treasury, and created a sculpted facsimile of Alexander for display in the glass coffin. This golden sheath containing Alexander's physical remains was hidden away in a secret tomb beneath the Serapeum where it remained undisturbed and was eventually forgotten." She looked over at him. "Until we found it and brought it here."

"Why the subterfuge?"

"An obvious explanation is that the priests revered Alexander and saw the emperor's actions as a desecration. However, our research has yielded a different explanation. Alexander's body is radioactive."

Kismet resisted the urge to recoil. Was that the energy he had been sensing? He knew he could almost instantly recover from most injuries, but radiation wasn't like a knife blade or a bullet. In fact, just the opposite, because his seeming immortality was the result of rapid cellular regeneration, and since gamma rays could wreak havoc on cellular nuclei, triggering potentially deadly mutations, his rapid-healing might actually promote an explosion of cancerous growths in him.

"Barely above the level of background radiation," Leda added. "Though two thousand years ago, it might have been cause for concern, if not for the shielding provided by this layer of gold." She paused a beat. "You are familiar, I take it, with the story of Alexander's death?"

"I know that he died young. In his thirties. From typhoid fever, if I recall correctly. Although some think he may have been poisoned."

"He was poisoned, but not by his rivals or enemies."

"Radiation poisoning."

Leda nodded. "He found the anomaly in Babylon, in the Esagila. The door to the secret chamber opened to him. It may be that he was indeed a descendant of the Ancients. There are many alive today who carry a trace of their DNA. Your father—your adoptive father, Christian Garral—for instance. And his grandfather, Adam Garral.

"Whether through experimentation or some arcane knowledge passed down through the ages, we cannot say, but Alexander recognized that the anomaly—this emerald—was a source of incredible power. He believed he could use it to produce an elixir which would not only give him immortality, but transform him into the god he already believed he was. Unfortunately for him, the process of creating the elixir released a lethal dose of radiation. History records his slow death of fever, but it does not record that those who ministered to him during that time also sickened and died. The priests however understood what was happening. That is why they refused to bring him into the temple. They knew he would not recover, and that anyone who came into contact with him would also be afflicted. They also knew that encasing Alexander's body in gold would protect them."

"His mistake was in attempting to create the elixir with only one of the anomalies in his possession," said Hauser, speaking for the first time since entering the vault. He still gripped the backpack by its straps, holding it suspended a few feet away from the golden figure.

"You're after the elixir?" Kismet shook his head. "Why? You're already immortal."

Hauser grinned. "You think that's all this is about? Tell me brother, have you read the text of the Tabula Smaragdina?"

Kismet had in fact read several different translations of the text.

Hauser went on. "It purports to contain the secret formula for creating *prima materia*—the First

Matter, from which all other material in the universe was created."

"You mean hydrogen?" Kismet shot back, with more than a little sarcasm.

"Ah, very good. You didn't sleep through your physics classes after all. In their own unique way, the Hermetical scholars of the past understood a rudimentary form of nuclear physics. The point of the formula was not to identify *prima materia*, but to create it out of nothingness, and subsequently to shape it into anything they desired—gold, healing medicines, what have you. That is what Alexander attempted to do, and it's what killed him."

"How did he manage that with just one of the elemental relics?" Kismet asked.

"Who knows? Maybe he tried using actual fire, earth and water." Hauser waved a dismissive hand. "What is certain is that the Emerald Tablet—not that crystal there, but the ancient Hermetic text, is the key to understanding how this may be done.

"'And, as all things have been and arose from one by the mediation of one; so all things have their birth from this one thing… The sun is its father, the moon its mother, the wind hath carried it in its belly, the earth is its nurse. The father of all perfection in the whole world is here. Its force or power is entire if it be converted into earth.' The original treatise on nuclear physics, translated by Sir Isaac Newton. But also, precise instructions for harnessing the power of creation itself, using the four anomalies.

"As you know, each of them represents an elemental force. What you call 'the Apex' symbolizes fire. Also, the sun or the Father. The orb I found in Antarctica is water, but is also the moon, the Mother."

Kismet knew that Maddock and Rose had actually been the ones to discover the orb, but he let Hauser have the credit. "I thought Earth was supposed to be our mother?"

"In the most ancient traditions, the moon was a goddess, and since the moon creates the tides which primarily affect the oceans, it seems clear that sun and moon represent fire and water respectively. Of course, the rest of the passage makes it clear. Wind and earth are plainly identified. The obsidian mirror is a symbol of earth, and that—" He pointed at the green crystal. "—is the symbol of air. The womb from which *prima materia* is born."

"Newton's translation gives precise instructions: 'Separate thou the earth from the fire, the subtle from the gross sweetly with great industry. It ascends from the earth to the heaven and again it descends to the earth and receives the force of things superior and inferior. By this means you shall have the glory of the whole world.'"

Kismet tried to parse the instructions. "Separating earth from fire sounds like nuclear fission."

"You're not thinking literally enough," Hauser

countered. "Newton was describing the physical arrangement of the anomalies."

The image of the Magus tarot card, which he had found in Adam Garral's journal, now flashed in Kismet's mind's eye—a divine magician, originally identified as the Roman god Mercury, but possibly a representation of Hermes Trismegistus, surrounded by elemental symbols, manipulating them like a juggler. "Earth and fire… The Apex and the Magna of Illusion. They have to be kept apart?"

"Not just kept apart. Newton's translation gives us a riddle. Separate the 'subtle' from the 'gross.' Of the two that remain, air and water, which would you describe as subtle?"

"Air?"

"I agree. Now the next part. 'It ascends from the earth to the heaven.' Logically, earth would be below fire and sky, so we would arrange the four elements vertically, with your Apex stone at the top. The emerald below it. Then the mirror, and lastly, the orb. 'By this means you shall have the glory of the whole world.' What do you say, brother? Give it a try?" He flashed a wolfish grin, and then swung the pack toward Kismet who caught it reflexively.

Kismet immediately felt the magnetic attraction between the relics and had to lean back a little to keep from being pulled off balance. As he stood there, fighting it, his earlier unease intensified into a feeling of wooziness, like vertigo. He shook his head. "This is your fantasy, not mine."

He adjusted his grip on the pack, preparing to

heave it back, but Hauser raised his hands in a halting gesture. "Oh, but I insist."

Suddenly Kismet understood the real reason Hauser had brought him along. "What's the matter, brother? Worried that maybe you aren't as immortal as you think you are?"

Hauser shrugged. "Why take the chance when I've got you here to do the heavy lifting for me?"

"Aren't you afraid of what I might do with this much power?" Kismet shot back.

Hauser grinned as if amused by the suggestion. "So much for the myth of the good son, eh, mother?" He kept his gaze focused on Kismet. "Really, brother, give me some credit. I left some of my men in Alexandria with instructions concerning your friends in Alexander's Tomb. If they don't hear from me in…" He made a show of checking his wristwatch, and then laughed. "Well, let's just say if they don't hear from me in the next half hour or so, they will detonate a rather large bomb at the entrance to the ruin. Help me and help your friends. Oppose me, and I guarantee, they will all die. Tick, tock, brother."

Kismet glanced over at their mother. Leda was watching with undisguised eagerness—her offspring, solving the secrets of creation in preparation to seize heaven itself. There was not a trace of concern in her expression. "Do it, Nick. You have the blood of titans in you. You will not be harmed."

Kismet sagged in defeat. He didn't expect

Hauser to keep his word with respect to freeing Maddock and the others, but until this moment, he had hoped to find a way to liberate one or all of the relics and escape. With this new threat, he was out of options. "I guess you've thought of everything," he muttered.

He curled one of the straps around his left forearm and then carefully unzipped the pack with his right hand.

Inside, the three relics were stuck together by the same magnetic attraction that was pulling them toward the emerald. The base of the Apex was perfectly centered on the obsidian mirror, which was in turn pressed flat against the sphere so that the peak of the blue pyramid talisman was pointing away from the emerald. The arrangement was too exact to be random or haphazard. The elemental relics were trying to align themselves, exactly as Hauser had described, but one was missing. The Apex—representing fire—was in contact with the Magna of Illusion—representing earth.

He reached in and tried to separate the two, but the attraction was too strong.

He recalled the instructions from the Emerald Tablet: Separate earth from the fire, the subtle from the gross sweetly with great industry.

Sweetly with great industry, he thought. *What the hell is that supposed to mean?*

"Hard work, I guess," he muttered. But how? He couldn't get enough leverage to do more than wiggle it.

But the answer was obvious.

In legend, Alexander had used his sword to cut the Gordian Knot, solving a complex problem with direct action—brute force. And in both the tarot deck and Kismet's vision of the Emerald Tablet, he had also seen Alexander's sword. Whether the story of the Gordian Knot was literal or allegorical, he could not say, but he understood that in order to separate earth from fire "sweetly with great industry" he was going to need the emerald.

He let the relics pull him closer to the golden coffin, feeling weaker with each step. He was no Superman, but the green crystal was affecting him like Kryptonite. And as he advanced, the attraction intensified, overpowering him, yanking him forward until the bag made contact with the emerald. As it did, the gem was ripped free of the sculpted hands, twisting away to shoot across the remaining distance. There was a distinctive clink as it pierced the fabric of the pack and made contact with the orb, sticking straight out like an arrow piercing an apple. As it did, the pack twisted around and dropped to the vault floor with the emerald pointing straight down. The backpack slid down the length of the emerald and settled into a shapeless heap around it, revealing all four elemental relics, joined together for possibly the first time ever. They remained upright, just barely touching the floor, perfectly balanced like a top or gyroscope, but without any spinning.

Kismet could feel energy radiating out from it— invisible, inaudible, but nevertheless palpable. It was sucking the life out of him. And he knew why. The relics were not aligned correctly. He would need to pry them apart, reassemble them in the correct order.

And if I do? What happens then?

He moved in closer, wrapping his left arm around the orb for leverage, and then gripped the Apex, pulling it with an effort that seemed to take the last of his waning strength. It resisted stolidly, as if the two relics had already fused together at the atomic level, but then, just when he was about to give up, it broke loose and came away in his hand.

He could feel it tugging against him, straining to be reunited with the others, like a powerful magnet, but the simple act of separating one piece of the puzzle seemed to reduce the weakening effect of the joined artifact. Without letting go, he reached down with the hand that held the Apex, and took hold of the emerald.

The green crystal refused to break contact, but he did manage to rotate it away from the floor.

Separate earth from fire… The emerald goes between the mirror and the Apex.

He slid the pyramid down the length of the crystal and placed it at the point opposite the orb. The Apex seemed to jump out of his hand, positioning itself with the point of the emerald exactly at the center.

He allowed himself a relieved sigh. He'd gotten that part right at least.

With one hand gripping the emerald and the other on the mirror, he began pulling, bringing the two objects together, scraping them across the outer surface of the orb until at last, they made contact. He maintained the pressure, lifting one edge of the mirror so that the other edge, the one closest to the tip of the emerald tilted down, and pushed the crystal up, onto the mirror—

The relic jolted in his hands, the emerald sliding to the center of the mirror as if suddenly realizing that was where it was meant to be. Immediately, the combined object flipped upright again, rotating in Kismet's grasp until the Apex was pointing straight up. Light began pulsing along the emerald, traveling down from the Apex and vanishing into the inky darkness of the Magna of Illusion, but after a moment, something like beads of mercury began appearing on the surface of the obsidian mirror, pooling together and running off the edge to drip down onto the orb. But instead of rolling down the curved surface of the large sphere, the beads vanished as if sucked up by a sponge. A few seconds later, the orb itself began to glow, like an enormous black light bulb. It was not a carbon-tungsten filament that was producing the illumination however, but rather a pool of shining quicksilver accumulating at the bottom of the sphere's interior.

There was one other significant change. Kismet could still feel invisible energy radiating out from the newly created object, but the timbre of it was different. No longer did he feel like it was draining the life out of him. Just the opposite, he felt an infusion of energy. Literal warmth, spread through his body, tingling in his extremities, growing unpleasantly hot inside his thermal winter garments.

Yet, the physical discomfort was the least of his concerns. He understood now what Hauser had hoped to accomplish.

By this means you shall have the glory of the whole world.

The elemental relics were creating *prima materia*—First Matter—the stuff from which the universe had been created.

The scientists of Prometheus had given it a different name however.

Ichor. The blood of the gods.

Fuel for an army of god-bodies.

16.

"**I told you** he went along with this just to save us," Jade whispered in Maddock's ear.

He shot her an angry look, a finger pressed to his lips, signaling her to silence, though it was plainly evident that nobody outside their little group had heard her.

Once past the electronic lock inside the entrance, they moved quickly into the vault. Most of the doors had been left open, as if Hauser's team could not be bothered to shut them.

A check of the security cameras still showed no sign of Hauser's group, but Rose's hatchet head, continued to point the way like a compass needle, and when the inner airlock door opened, the mystery was solved. Although positioned in such a way as to be uncovered by the security cameras, the entire back wall of the vault had swung open to reveal another chamber. And in that vault they found wonders beyond comprehension. There were display cases containing objects of incredible beauty and obvious wealth—crowns and amulets, scepters and swords, but the most impressive part of the collection were the statues. There were at least two dozen of them, assembled in ranks like the terracotta armies found in the tomb of Chinese emperor Qin Shi Huang, except these were each eight to ten feet in height, towering over Maddock, and appeared to be made of solid gold. The statues were remarkably lifelike, depicting well-muscled male and voluptuous female figures, all of them exuding power and sensuality. They reminded Maddock of sculpted Greek gods.

The biggest surprise however had been the voices that drifted through the forest of towering metal figures. Maddock and the others had crept forward, close enough to observe what was happening without being noticed, though in fact, the group huddled around the golden coffin were so completely focused on the powerful elemental relics, and the task of arranging them according to ancient Hermetic wisdom, that Maddock and the others might as well have been in an alternate universe.

Jade was correct, though. Kismet was going along with Hauser's plan because he believed their safety was at stake.

They had to let him know that Hauser's threat was a bluff, but how?

A few well-placed shots would thin out the opposition, but once the shooting started, there was no telling what would happen. Then there was the fact that Hauser had control of the relics and knew how to use them. He might easily deflect their attack with a force field or roast them all with lightning bolts.

Then fate decided to give them a break. Hauser handed the backpack with the relics to Kismet.

"What's he doing?" Bones muttered.

"Maybe he's worried about radiation

poisoning," suggested Rose. "Maybe that's the one thing that can kill him."

"Good to know," Bones said.

"Then it can kill Nick, too," Christian Garral said, his voice betraying his anxiety. "And us if we get too close."

Maddock studied the group gathered around Alexander's coffin. There was no question regarding the loyalties of the five gunmen but what about Leda? Whose side was she on?

Judging by her interactions with her two sons, the answer was her own.

"We need to break this party up." He turned his head to Bones. "Think you could create some kind of distraction? Something that might draw a few of those guys away?"

"Divide and conquer?" Bones eyes narrowed in thought then a broad grin spread across his face. "I know exactly what to do."

"Professor, you go with him. When you're in position, break squelch on the radio. I'll signal back when we're ready for you to go, and then I'll send you the number of targets headed your way. Voice if I can, but if not, I'll key the mic with the number."

Bones nodded and then turned to Professor. "You're gonna love this."

As the two men moved off, Maddock returned his attention to what was happening below. Kismet had neared the golden coffin and was struggling to align the relics. That they were having a harmful effect on him was plainly evident.

"What's your plan?" asked Garral.

Maddock quickly outlined what he needed Garral and the others to do, and then waited with the Motorola pressed to his ear, the volume just barely loud enough for him to hear the scratch of static when Bones signaled that he was in position.

Maddock gave a hand-signal to the others to get ready, and then clicked the push-to-talk and whispered, "Do it!"

For several seconds, nothing happened at all. Directly ahead, Kismet had succeeded in rearranging the elemental artifacts, and the subsequent change almost caused Maddock to forget about the plan.

The orb had turned semi-transparent and appeared to be filling up with a substance that looked like liquid light.

Suddenly, a crashing sound—like a bus hitting a brick wall—reverberated through the vault. A fraction of a second later, there was another crash, and then another, each one progressively louder. Hauser's group were visibly startled by the noises. So was Maddock.

Bones, what the hell did you just do?

He got the answer a couple crashes later when he spied movement among the statues off to his left. They were toppling over like bowling pins, with each one striking one or two more as it fell in a chain reaction. Maddock wasn't sure how Bones had managed to start the domino effect—each of the statues must have weighed tons—but once begun, there was no stopping it.

The coffin at the center was a few yards removed from the impact zone, but the gunmen nevertheless retreated a few steps. Each impact released a shockwave that vibrated through the floor and buffeted the air. Even after the last affected statue fell, the echoes of the crashes continued to reverberate in the large vault in a deafening cacophony.

Yet, through it all, Nick Kismet did not move. He stood frozen, statue-still, as if in a trance, while beads of glowing energy perspired from the obsidian mirror and were absorbed into the orb.

Hauser was gesturing to his men, shouting words that were inaudible over the ongoing tumult, and three of them moved off, presumably to investigate the disturbance. They approached the statues cautiously,

As the three gunmen disappeared behind the statues, moving warily as if fearing another round of collapses, Maddock broke squelch three times, hoping Bones would get the message. He waited a few more seconds, and then raised his hand. "Now!"

In unison, Maddock and the others emerged from their hiding places, each one of them aiming a weapon at a designated target. Maddock took aim at Hauser and shouted, "Guns down! Nobody move!"

Maddock had instructed his companions to fire at the first sign of aggression, but hoped a display of force would suffice to win the battle without a shot fired. It wasn't that he was squeamish about bloodshed, but rather because there was no telling what might happen if bullets started flying. Garral seemed to know how to handle firearms, but Rose, Jade and Jimmy looked far less comfortable with their weapons, and if they missed or merely hesitated, their slight numerical advantage would evaporate.

Hauser whirled around, surprise quickly giving way to anger. "Maddock!"

The two remaining gunmen had tensed but wisely had not attempted to raise their weapons.

"I mean it," Maddock said, holding the weapon steady, Hauser's face visible just above the luminous Trijicon dot on the front sight. "Make the wrong move and you're dead. That may not mean anything to you, Hauser, but I'm betting your men might feel differently. Now, get those hands up. All of you."

As the two gunmen grudgingly complied, Maddock took another step forward and risked a quick glance past Hauser to where Kismet was standing. "Nick, you all right?"

Kismet did not answer right away, prompting Maddock to repeat the question. This time, he got a reply. "Stay back," Kismet rasped. "It's not safe."

No kidding, Maddock thought. Aloud, he said, "We need to get out of here."

"It's not that simple. This thing is making *ichor.*"

Maddock knew the word from Greek mythology. *Ichor* was the blood that flowed through the veins of the gods. He wasn't sure what it meant in this context, but it was obviously something bad. "You've got the relics, so you're calling the shots."

"Get everyone out of here. Now that I know you're all safe—"

The crack of rifle fire cut him off. It hadn't come from nearby but from somewhere out in the vault—several shots in quick succession, and not all from the same kind of weapon. Bones and Professor had engaged with the three gunmen who had gone to investigate the toppling of the statues.

The remaining two men flinched and began looking around anxiously, as if weighing their chances at attempting some kind of offensive action, but it was Hauser who ultimately seized the moment. Maddock squeezed the trigger, knowing that his shot would only temporarily take Hauser out of action, but he was a fraction of a second too slow. Hauser ducked under the bullet and sprang at Kismet. In the same instant, the two gunmen broke in opposite directions, seeking cover behind the fallen statues, firing their assault rifles on the move.

Pandemonium erupted in the vault. Bullets were sizzling through the air, sparking off solid surfaces or whizzing harmlessly away into nothingness. Maddock dropped low, quickly assessing his options. There weren't many. He tackled Leda to the floor, drawing her behind the relative cover of the bier containing Alexander's coffin. He didn't know whose side she was on, but figured she was more valuable alive than dead.

He came up on one knee searching for a target, and from the corner of his eye, saw Kismet and Hauser struggling, with the combined elemental relic caught between them. The object wasn't affixed to anything, yet it remained upright and immobile, as solid as a flagpole, while the two men wrestled for control.

He felt Kismet's eyes on him and glanced over. The man was shouting something, barely audible over the thunder of battle.

"Get out of here!"

Maddock didn't know what Kismet was planning, but the advice was sound. He gripped Leda's hand and pulled her after him, making a break for the edge of the circle of statues where the others were waiting. He was faintly aware of a shift in fire, Jimmy and Garral trying to suppress any action from the shooters as best they could with their bolt-action rifles. He made it just halfway before a brilliant flash—light and heat—from behind him filled the vault, followed almost immediately by a shockwave that slapped him flat, sending him and Leda sprawling.

He thought it had to be an explosion, maybe a hand grenade, but there had been no sound. In fact, even the gunfire close in had ceased. Shaking off the effects of the blast, he scrambled back to his feet. Leda was still down, dazed, but as Maddock reached for her, he saw her gaze flash back to where they had just been. Where her sons were battling for control of the elemental talisman.

Maddock looked as well, and instantly saw what had caused the flash.

At first glance, it appeared that Kismet had ceded control of the relic to Hauser. The latter had both arms wrapped around the relic while Kismet had not only let go but had retreated a few steps.

But there was something different about the relic. It was no longer vibrating at the same frequency as before, nor was *ichor* pooling on the surface of the mirror. In fact, the Magna of Illusion was no longer in contact with the emerald. Instead, it seemed as if the orb and mirror had rotated upside down so that the emerald, still topped with the Apex, was protruding directly from the top of the sphere, while the mirror was now at its bottom.

Maddock immediately realized what had happened. Kismet had pried the emerald away from the obsidian mirror, breaking whatever kind of circuit had been created. That had been the source of the eruption that had flattened Maddock. The relic had then reassembled itself in a different order.

Hauser's hands were moving frantically, trying to separate the relics and undo what Kismet had done, but he was already too late. The orb was expelling the fiery substance that had been accumulating inside it. Glowing ichor was oozing from the mirror, accumulating into a fat molten globule underneath the elemental relic.

Kismet snatched something off the ground—

Rose's backpack—and thrust a hand inside. When he withdrew it, he was holding his *kukri.* Without a moment's hesitation, he leaped at his brother, swiping the knife in a broad lateral arc. Hauser's eyes went wide and he ducked away. Instead of taking his head off, only the tip of the blade made contact, gouging a line of red across the man's cheek. As Hauser let go of his prize, dancing away to avoid another slash of the *kukri,* the growing blob of *ichor* fell away, but it did not hit the floor. Instead, it burst like a bubble, evaporating into a glittering cloud that rose into the air and then, as if caught in a vacuum, dispersed in all directions.

Maddock's attention was still fixed on Kismet and Hauser, so he only caught a glimpse of the *ichor* mist settling onto the statues, briefly condensing into droplets on their metal surface before being absorbed. But when he spotted motion from the corner of his eye, he turned his head for a better look.

It was no mere optical illusion, no trick of the light. All around him, the giant golden figures were beginning to stir.

17.

The statues moved slowly at first, like sleepers dragging themselves up to consciousness. Their golden exterior was as supple as actual skin, allowing smooth, unrestricted motion, such that the only sound was of heavy hands thudding against the solid concrete floor as the fallen statues began struggling to right themselves. Those that had survived Bones' diversion without being toppled simply straightened and began milling about.

Watching them, Maddock searched for some indication that they were truly alive, but saw none. They seemed more like animatronic figures than living beings.

Animatronic figures as big as elephants and evidently, completely independent.

His observation was cut short by a burst from an assault rifle. He swung his eyes in the direction of the muzzle flash, and saw one of Hauser's men, surrounded by the shuffling figures. Bullets stitched one of the statues, but instead of cratering the soft metal, the rounds vanished into it like a pebble thrown into a pond. There were even ripples of energy spreading out from the points of impact, meeting and canceling one another out.

Yet, as impotent as the attack proved to be, it got the attention of the animated statues. Those nearest the gunman immediately swung to face him.

Perhaps sensing his imminent peril, the man tried to flee the circle, but a golden hand shot out from his blind side and plucked him off the ground. The statue—a male figure with curly hair and beard—lifted the gunman like a doll and dashed him to the floor. Maddock heard the crunch of the man's bones breaking. Immediately, the other statues raised their fists above the shattered form, and then with what seemed like mechanical efficiency, proceeded to pound the man into a bloody pulp.

Another flurry of motion distracted Maddock. He glanced toward it and saw Hauser's retreating back disappear into the midst of another cluster of statues. Kismet was close on his brother's heels, his *kukri* still bared and ready for action. Only then did Maddock realize that the elemental relic was gone, taken presumably by Hauser as he fled. Kismet reached the statues a moment later, and then he too disappeared as the statues turned to follow, ponderous but relentless.

Maddock grabbed Leda's wrist and began moving away from the vault's center, and away from the unfolding carnage. He could feel the eyes of some of the statues turning toward him, following his movements, shifting toward him as if drawn to any motion, but he did not stop. Off to his left, he heard another burst of gunfire—the other gunman—which was just as quickly cut off. The swift reprisal seemed to confirm his working theory that the statues were at their most lethal when attacked.

"Don't shoot at them!" he shouted, straining to make himself heard over the thud and crunch of another pulverization-in-progress. Still gripping his pistol, he awkwardly unclipped his radio and squeezed the push-to-talk. "Bones! Do not engage those things. Get out of the vault."

He didn't wait for a response, but kept moving, heading for the spot where he'd left the others. He spotted Garral and Rose. The two were poised like running backs on a football field, watching for the opening that would allow them to make a break for the end zone. He found Jade and Jimmy nearby, similarly dodging the giant automatons as they shifted this way and that, moving far slower than those that had killed the gunmen.

"Get to the exit!" he shouted as he got near the others. "And whatever you do, don't attack them!"

"Which way?" asked Jade, ducking to avoid a slow swipe from a tall Aphrodite.

The question confounded Maddock. In the confusion, he had become disoriented, and with the statues now in motion, milling about and blocking his view of the vault's edges, he had no idea which direction to go.

Leda chose that moment to pull free of his grip, but she did not flee. Instead, she just stood there at arm's length, massaging her wrist where Maddock had held it. She met his gaze and then looked to his left. "That way."

Maddock was about to thank her, but just then

something struck his cheek. It was cold and hard, like a hailstone.

No, not like. It *was* hail. Tiny pellets of ice were falling all around him, bouncing off his parka, rattling tinnily on the statues, or just splattering wetly on the floor.

Wet? He looked down and saw that this impression was indeed correct. The little hailstones were melting on the floor, leaving big damp splotches on the concrete.

"What's happening?" Rose shouted over the increasing patter.

"The *ichor* is raising the temperature in here," Leda said. There was no urgency in her tone. She might simply have been commenting on the weather. "It's thawing the permafrost."

The air was still cold enough to freeze the meltwater as it dripped down from the ceiling, but judging by the swiftness with which it melted again on the floor, the temperature was continuing to rise. The hail was now more like wet sleet, and coming down harder.

As if they didn't have enough to worry about.

"We've got to move," Maddock said. "If we get soaked, we'll freeze solid when we get outside."

"Maddock! Bring your ass!" Bones' voice reached out to him—not a radio transmission, but a shout. Through the haze of falling precipitation, Maddock could just make out his friend's towering form, one arm raised and waving him on.

Maddock saw something else, too. Something that Bones had missed. He pointed, frantic. "Bones! Behind you!"

Bones turned just in time to see a towering Zeus-like figure, one lazy hand reaching toward him. Bones started to pivot away, but before he could, something slammed down onto the statue, crushing it to the floor. A boulder, as big as a car, had fallen onto the golden automaton, flattening it. The impact jolted the floor and sent Bones sprawling toward Maddock, but he scrambled back to his feet as more mud and debris began to pour down from the melting permafrost ceiling.

Kismet ducked under a reaching hand, narrowly avoiding it, then dropped to his knees and slid between the legs of the titanic figure. Ice pellets were falling from the ceiling, melting into a slushy mess underfoot, which made the slide easy but recovering from it a lot trickier.

The vault was definitely warming up, the permafrost thawing, but that situation, like the rampage of the reanimated statues, had to take a back seat to his pursuit of Hauser. He popped back up just as Hauser cut to the right, disappearing behind another pillar-like leg. He was weaving through the god-bodies like a pinball, trying to shake his pursuer. Encumbered as he was by the elemental relic, the best he could do was to stay a few steps ahead, but with the statues running interference, a few steps was all he needed.

The golden giants were moving faster, reacting to them as they had to the attack by the gunmen. Their rampage was mindless. The *ichor* energized their bodies, but without the consciousness of the entities that had once occupied them, they were simply reacting according to some kind of primitive default behavior written into whatever they had that passed for a brain. Their actions reminded Kismet of warrior ants, swarming in response to a threat. But what was driving them to attack him? He wondered if it was the close proximity of the relic. Were they drawn to it, recognizing it as the source of their potent lifeblood? Or was Hauser using it to control them somehow? Either way, Kismet knew that getting the relic back, separating the pieces and scattering them once more to the four winds was of paramount importance. If Hauser escaped the vault with the relic, there was no telling what kind of hell he might unleash on the world.

Kismet spotted the open vault door through a forest of legs as tall as he was. If he could get there before Hauser….

Too late. His brother was already there, his silhouette starkly visible against the whiteness of the seed vault beyond. Hauser seemed to hesitate there, just for a second, then he was gone, disappearing down the aisle between the empty racks.

As he reached the opening a moment later,

Kismet saw the reason for his brother's pause. The false walls that served as a secret entrance to the Prometheus vault were swinging closed. They were moving too slow to prevent him from slipping through, but even as he did, he realized the true reason Hauser had done this.

Kismet might be able to make it out, but his companions would be imprisoned inside, trapped with an army of mindlessly destructive automatons.

He looked back, searching for some sign of Maddock and the others, but all he saw through the blur of precipitation were gigantic golden figures stalking relentlessly toward him.

"Damn it," he muttered. This was why he preferred operating solo.

He returned his attention to Hauser, who was now more than halfway to the airlock door, and knew what he had to do. He took off down the aisle at a full sprint.

The only way to help the others was to stop his brother, get the relic back. If he didn't he would almost certainly have a lot more deaths on his conscience. Besides, he wasn't even sure he would be able to stop the door from closing, or get it open again once it was shut. His mother might know, and she was in there, too.

That realization only added to his growing sense of guilt.

Even though it was the right choice, the only choice, it felt like he was abandoning them all to an uncertain fate. Alexandria all over again, only worse.

Fifty feet ahead, Hauser was past the steel safety cage. He slammed the gate shut behind him with such force that it rebounded halfway open again, but he was already gone, shooting toward the airlock doors.

Kismet blasted through the gate just as Hauser entered the airlock and pulled the door shut, practically slamming it in his brother's face. Kismet had too much momentum to stop and crashed into the doors. The impact rattled his teeth and he bounded back, spilling painfully onto the floor, but he was up again in a heartbeat, reaching for the lever.

Locked.

He rattled it repeatedly, knowing that it would disengage as soon as the outer door was closed again. *Unless Hauser wedged it open,* he thought.

Unwilling to wait and see, he jammed the point of his *kukri* into the gap between the doors and attempted to pry them apart. The thick blade was more than tough enough to serve double-duty as a crowbar, but he wasn't just fighting the lock. The rising temperatures had increased the already slightly higher air pressure in the vault, forcing them to remain shut. He tried to drive the knife in deeper, but his gloved hand slipped off the hilt, sliding along the length of the blade. He winced as the edge slice through Gore-tex and skin alike, and snatched his hand back in an instinctive protective reflex. Blood was already seeping through the gash in the glove, dripping down to stain the floor in dark red blotches.

He bit down on the finger of the glove and yanked it off. Blood was streaming from the gash, but he wiped it on the front of his parka. His hand was throbbing all the way up to his elbow. Rapid healing abilities did not grant him any immunity from pain, but he gritted his teeth and did his best to ignore it as he resumed trying to force the doors open.

A loud crash filled the vault, shaking the floor and dislodging a shower of ice chunks from the ceiling above. The accompanying shock wave buffeted Kismet, shoving him forward and nearly knocking him down again.

A glance over his shoulder confirmed what he already knew had happened. Through the parallel rows of shelves, he could see an uneven gap in the back wall. The god-bodies were smashing through it. If the walls of the vault would not contain them, nothing would. Before he could turn back to his task, there was another resounding crash and one of the golden forms stumbled forward into the empty seed vault where it immediately began shoving shelving racks out of the way, intent on clearing a path for the exit.

Kismet whipped his head back around, desperate to get the airlock doors open. To his astonishment, he discovered this had already been accomplished. The tremors had shaken the doors off their hinges. He bolted through, and kept going, past the still-open exterior doors. He made the turn and headed back to the long tunnel leading up to the surface where he finally caught sight of his brother, just for a moment as the latter slipped through the door at the far end.

He sprinted ahead, crossing the full distance in about thirty seconds. He was surprised at how winded the effort left him. His brief exposure to the relic in its correct alignment had not, it seemed, completely recharged his batteries. Nevertheless, he dug deep and poured everything into catching his brother.

As he burst through the last set of doors, emerging into the darkness of the Arctic at midday, he heard the diminishing whine of a snowmobile engine. A white plume trailed out behind a dark speck shooting away, straight down the hill, toward the not-so-distant lights of the airport and the plane that would carry Hauser away, along with a power that might reshape the world.

Or destroy it.

Without a moment's hesitation, Kismet jumped on one of the remaining snowmobiles, started it, and took off after his brother.

18.

It was quickly apparent that the golden giants had lost all interest in Maddock and the others. That was the good news. The bad news was that the animated statues were now clustered around the only exit from the vault—a breach they had forced in the false walls separating the Prometheus vault from the empty seed vault.

The even worse news was that the permafrost overhead was melting fast and coming down even faster.

Maddock had one arm raised overhead to ward off falling rocks and mud. It was a symbolic effort but at least it kept the mud out of his eyes.

"When I heard this place was called the Doomsday Vault, I thought it meant something else," Bones said, shouting to be heard over the din. He looked past Maddock to the line of stragglers behind him. "Where's Kismet?"

"He took off," Maddock said. He knew there was more to the story, but once again, their new *friend* had made a unilateral decision and abandoned them all.

Bones evidently felt the same way. "Again? Screw that guy. He's off the team." He glanced over at Christian Garral and Leda Hauser and shrugged. "Sorry, but you're kid's a dick."

Garral grimaced, apologetically, but Leda's face

was an emotionless mask.

"There's Professor," Jade shouted, pointing in the direction of the logjam at the exit, and to a figure huddling in the relative shelter of the wall nearby.

Bones nodded. "I hope he can figure out how we're gonna get through that mess 'cause I got nothing."

As if to mock his hopelessness, the mass of statues surged again and then, like a shower of champagne behind a loosened cork, exploded through the hole. beyond the opening, Maddock could see the statues continuing their destructive rampage, trashing the shelves in the empty vault. The giants were still between them and freedom, but at least the way out of the Prometheus vault was clear.

Behind them, huge chunks of the ceiling continued to crash down, obliterating what little remained of the collection and splattering the fleeing group with cold mud, but as they cautiously started through into the seed vault, something changed.

The statues' movements were growing sluggish. Some were squatting on their haunches or kneeling amidst the ruin of the seed vault as if uncertain what to do next. One of them—a male figure—took a tentative step toward the exit, but then froze in place.

"The *ichor* is depleting," Leda said, pushing

forward.

Beside Maddock, Bones muttered. "Translation: Dead batteries."

"Not dead enough," Maddock said. "We need to get past them."

Easier said than done. The giants had transformed the seed vault into a nightmarish obstacle course. The neat orderly rows of shelving were broken and scattered across the floor, and the steel posts that had supported them were bent and twisted around the slow-moving statues like tentacles. Worse, the warming effect had followed the giants, and despite the refrigeration system, ice and chunks of melting permafrost were starting to fall from the ceiling.

Maddock glanced back to make sure everyone else was still with him. "Watch your step," he advised, "And keep your head on a swivel."

With that admonition, he started forward, picking his way over the tangled metal and ducking slow swipes from the giants. He guessed their dwindling power supply would be completely exhausted in another two or three minutes, but they couldn't afford to wait and see. Not only was the vault still coming down around them, there was an even bigger problem. Hauser had possession of the elemental relics. Despite his irritation with Kismet's decision to leave them all behind, he knew why the man had done it. It was bad enough that Hauser seemed to be unkillable. They couldn't afford to let him add "omnipotent" to his resume.

He reached the far end of the vault without mishap, noting the drops of blood that were freezing on the floor, and kept going. There were more bloodstains on the floor, a trail leading all the way back to the front door and beyond. Someone had been injured during the escape from the vault, and the dark drops showed exactly where they had gone.

The air outside, cooler than in the vault room, quickly froze the mud on his coat and snow pants into a crust that crackled as he ran. Thankfully, the waterproof outer shell of the garments had resisted saturation.

Although the snowmobiles were too far away for him to hear them, their headlamps showed their location and progress. The lead vehicle—almost certainly Hauser—was halfway to the airport, the second machine—Kismet—trailing by about a hundred yards.

Maddock ran to one of the two remaining snowmobiles. Bones landed in the saddle of the other. He knew there was almost no chance of either of them catching Hauser, but Kismet was almost close enough. Almost.

Maddock searched the line of figures emerging from the seed vault until he identified Professor. "Prof! Can you do something with that rifle?"

The other man squinted into the distance. "I doubt I can hit him."

Jimmy piped in. "Let me take a crack at it. I'm pretty good with a sniper rifle."

Maddock gaped at him. "Since when?"

Professor rolled his eyes. "Video games."

Maddock shook his head, more an expression of disbelief than denial. "Whatever. You don't need to hit him. Just give him something to think about. Keep him away from the airport. Buy us some time."

Maddock hit the starter and the snowmobile roared to life. He goosed the throttle until the skis fell into the trail left by the other two machines, and then opened it wide.

The wind chilled his unprotected face, pelting him with ice crystals that stung his cheeks. He had to squint to keep from being blinded. His only consolation was that the ordeal would not last long. It would only take a few minutes to cover the distance to the airport.

Hauser was already almost there.

The rifle report cracked overhead, loud enough for him to hear it over the engine noise and the rush of air. Another followed quickly. Then another. Jimmy and Professor were alternating their shots, setting up a constant, if slow-tempo, barrage of suppressive fire. He couldn't tell where the bullets were hitting, but evidently they were close enough. Further down the hill, the headlights of the lead snowmobile abruptly veered to the right.

Maddock risked opening his eyes a little wider, tracking the course correction. Hauser was zigzagging, carving a wavy line in the snow, but with each left turn, he pushed closer to the illuminated runway. Up on the hill, Jimmy and Professor seemed to realize what the other man intended; not only did they intensify the rate of fire whenever Hauser shifted back to the left, they also appeared to be directing their shots closer, adjusting their aim and dialing in on the moving target. Accurate or not, the constant fire was having the desired effect. Hauser's evasive maneuvers had cut his lead on Kismet by half, and Maddock and Bones were closing quickly as well.

Without letting go of the throttle, Maddock reached up, unclipped his walkie-talkie and held it against his ear. "Bones, you still with me?"

Bones' voice crackled back a moment later. "Right on your ass. Gotta say, the view sucks."

Maddock suppressed a chuckle. "Then let's change it up a little? I'm gonna sweep wide-right. Try to push him back toward you."

"Gotcha," was all Bones said.

Maddock immediately veered off the blazed trail, plunging into the untrammeled snow. It was like floating on a cloud. Over the top of the waist-high accumulation, he could just make out Bones' snowmobile, charging straight down the hill, and further out, two pinpoints of light—the headlights of Hauser's and Kismet's machines—drifting across the horizon in front of him, getting closer as he moved to intercept.

Hauser must have realized what he was attempting. After a few seconds, he veered back in the other direction, but his window of opportunity had already closed. He was past the airport and running headlong toward the open water of the fjord beyond.

Maddock stood up for a better look and saw Kismet, closing fast on Hauser, driving him relentlessly forward. Bones had swept to the left, cutting off any escape in that direction. Directly ahead, the white snowscape ended abruptly, marking the transition from ice to water.

"We got this bastard," Bones shouted over the radio. "He's got nowhere to go."

Maddock felt a twinge of apprehension. Hauser was like a cornered rat; with no avenues left for escape, his only option would be to fight, and with all four of the elemental relics in his possession, he would be more than a match for all of them.

Hauser had evidently reached the same conclusion. His snowmobile slowed and came to a full stop less than twenty yards from the water's edge, but he did not dismount. Instead, he remained in his seat, wrestling with the burden he had carried out of the Prometheus vault, fighting to pry the individual relics apart in order to assemble them in the correct order so he could use it to blast them all to oblivion.

Something flashed into Maddock's view. It was Kismet on his snowmobile, still running at full speed in pursuit of his brother.

He's not going to stop, Maddock realized.

Kismet didn't stop, but he launched himself off

the snowmobile at the last instant, rolling away as the riderless machine kamikazed into Hauser's vehicle.

From his vantage a hundred yards away and closing, Maddock saw the two snowmobiles come apart in an eruption of shattered fiberglass, metal and smoke, and then a second later, heard and felt the impact.

Maddock kept the throttle wide-open, charging toward the smoldering wreckage. The snow around the site of the collision was dark with oil stains and pieces of debris, but despite the violence of the crash, he knew better than to count Hauser out of the fight. He spotted Kismet, evidently unhurt, shaking off the effects of his tumble in the snow, then he saw something that caused him to let go of the throttle and slam on the brakes.

A dark hole had opened up under one of the broken snowmobiles, swallowing it completely.

He saw Bones approaching from the other direction and started waving frantically to get the other man's attention. Remembering the radio, he keyed the mic and shouted, "Back off. There's thin ice here. We're over water."

Bones must have gotten the message because he immediately turned away, heading back toward the lights of the airport.

Maddock knew he should probably do the same. Most of the fjord was ice free but evidently land ice had crept out over the water to form a shelf along the coastline. The mass was thick enough to support the weight of the snowmobiles, or rather it had been until the crash. Now there was no telling how much longer it would remain solid beneath him. Reasoning that he'd have a better chance of making it off the ice shelf on foot, he dismounted and cautiously started toward the wreck site. He found Kismet again and waved his arms. "Nick. Over here."

Kismet's head turned toward him but before he could reply, a grinning form materialized out of the darkness behind him. It was Hauser, and in his hands, the elemental relic—re-configured as it had been in the Prometheus vault—was beginning to glow.

Maddock threw out both hands in a plaintive gesture. "Stop. You'll melt the—"

An ear-splitting crack cut him off, and then the entire section of ice under all three of them came apart.

19.

Maddock threw himself flat, spread-eagling to distribute his weight. Hauser had vanished completely, dropping through the newly created fissure like a stone. Kismet, thrown off balance by the upset, tried to crawl away from the edge, but the ice beneath him gave out, plunging him into the frigid water as well. He thrashed on the surface for a moment, struggling to pull himself back onto the newly created floe. As he clawed for a purchase, his bare right hand left dark splotches on the white ice—fresh blood from an open wound—but the frozen surface crumbled at his touch, and as the water infiltrated his clothes he was dragged under.

"Crap!" Maddock snarled, knowing what he had to do.

Without leaving his prone position, he shrugged out of his parka and kicked off his boots. After the exertion of the escape from the vault and the subsequent snowmobile chase, the rush of cool air was refreshing for a second or two, but then the bitter edge seeped through his thermal undershirt and his muscles began clenching, drawing in against his torso, an automatic reaction to preserve body heat.

"Crap," he muttered again. "This is gonna suck."

The worst part was, he knew exactly how bad it would suck, but he nevertheless planted his palms on the icy surface and propelled himself ahead, sliding on his belly like a penguin. As he neared the edge, the ice floe tilted down with his weight, dropping him into the frigid sea.

The effects of immersion in nearly-freezing water on the human body were well understood by medical science. Many of the immediate reactions were involuntary, but some were not. Survival depended on knowing the difference and acting accordingly. Initial exposure—cold shock—was the most dangerous part. Cold receptors in the skin would trigger immediate physiological responses, beginning with a "gasp" reflex.

Maddock made sure to keep his head up, his face clear of the water as he went in to avoid drowning as the cold water washed over him, triggering that sudden inhalation.

Next came uncontrollable hyperventilation, a heart rate increase, and a spike in blood pressure— all of it, a natural response to hostile temperature, but potentially fatal, especially to those with a weak constitution. After the initial gasp, one of the next big dangers was giving in to panic, which in tandem with the involuntary urge to hyperventilate, could severely limit the oxygen supply, causing a person to black out.

Maddock knew that the effects would subside quickly, usually peaking with the first minute of exposure, but he also knew that Kismet, who was experiencing the same symptoms, but already underwater, did not have a minute.

He forced himself to hyperventilate even faster for a moment, trying to override the involuntary response, and then stopped and drew in as deep a breath as his chest would allow. Then, he rolled forward and dove into the water, aiming for the spot where he thought Kismet had gone down.

He knew that if he couldn't find Kismet on that first breath, he wouldn't get another chance, so he threw his arms wide, sweeping them back and forth, kicking to propel himself deeper. He had expected everything to be pitch black under the ice, and so it took a few seconds for his chill-addled brain to process the fact that there was a pale glow rising up from the depths.

It was the relic, still generating *ichor* despite being totally submerged.

In the instant that he realized it, the glow intensified to near solar brilliance, the lighting up the world beneath the ice like daylight. Maddock couldn't bear to look directly at it, but as he turned away, he spotted a blurry silhouette drifting nearby.

Maddock kicked toward the shape, hooked it with an arm. He could tell by the feel that it was a body—Kismet's body—still twitching, fighting to survive the double-punch of cold shock and drowning. Maddock reversed his position in the water, turning away from the radiance below, and began kicking hard to reach the surface. Before he'd gone even a few feet, the light abruptly went out.

Maddock didn't know what to make of the

development, and in truth, he barely retained the mental capacity to care. His arms and legs felt oddly detached. He could only tell that he was still holding on to Kismet by the amount of drag he was experiencing in trying to reach the surface. A moment later, he broke through and was welcomed by an icy chill that froze the water on his skin into stinging ice crystals. He kept kicking until Kismet emerged beside him, gasping and still struggling to stay afloat.

It took him a few seconds to orient toward shore, seconds in which he slid ever closer to the threshold of hypothermia. Simply getting out of the water wasn't going to be enough to save them. If anything, the water temperature—just above freezing—was warmer than the air above, so getting to shelter, somewhere warm, was imperative.

"Maddock!" Bones' shout rolled across the dark water. The big man was crouched at the edge of the broken ice shelf, waving frantically. "Over here."

Maddock began kicking toward him, paddling with his free hand, but Kismet was like an anchor. "Swim, damn it!" he gasped. "Swim or I'll leave you behind."

"Do it," Kismet coughed. "Leave me."

So much for the motivational speech, Maddock thought. "Forget it. Just swim."

Kismet broke free of his hold, pushing away, and immediately sank again, but Maddock snared the other man's wrist and kept swimming. Bones was just a couple yards away, then a few feet. A few inches.

Bones reached out and snagged him under the arm, dragging him up onto the ice, and Kismet with him. The cold air left him almost completely paralyzed, barely able to breathe, but he remained fully conscious, fully aware, as Bones dragged him and Kismet back to the snowmobile

"You know it's a good thing you managed to fish yourself out," Bones grumbled as he slung both of them across the passenger seat. "Because no way in hell was I gonna go in there after you."

He stripped off his parka and covered them with it, then rubbed his arms vigorously. "Brrr. You know what, next time a job takes us anywhere that requires long johns, you just count me out."

"Bones," Maddock said, struggling to get the words past his chattering teeth. "Just drive."

20.

When the fog of cold finally receded, allowing him to think more or less coherently, Maddock sat up and looked around. He immediately recognized his surroundings—the sleeping cabin of Garral's chartered jet. He was in one of the small beds, stripped naked but concealed under several layers of blankets.

He sat up and looked around, spotted Nick Kismet, similarly covered up, but otherwise looking no worse for wear, thanks, no doubt, to his extraordinary regenerative abilities.

"Welcome back to the land of the living warm," Kismet said, smiling.

Maddock chuckled. "Still hate the desert?"

Kismet inclined his head. "Maybe I'm hating it a little less." He rolled a coffee mug between his palms, one of which, Maddock noted, was wrapped in a thick gauze bandage. He recalled the blood trail in the vault, and the red stain on the crumbling ice just before Kismet had gone in. Kismet's immortality appeared to be wearing off.

Maddock also remembered Hauser's reluctance to manipulate the elemental relics personally. Perhaps he had known, or at least suspected, that the radiation from the combined artifact might have exactly such an effect.

If so, then maybe Hauser had lost his

invincibility as well.

Maybe he was truly dead, this time.

One can hope, Maddock thought.

He sat up a little higher. "So what did I miss? Where's everyone else?"

"Sleeping I think. We've been in the air for a few hours. Dad thought it would be better for us to get out of town before the local authorities got involved. Leda..." He hesitated. "My mother stayed behind to run interference for us. At least, that's what she said. She's probably doing damage control for Prometheus, hiding the existence of the secret vault and recovering whatever she can."

There was a note of bitterness in his tone, as if, despite their evident success in thwarting Hauser, they had been handed a defeat.

"What about the relics?"

Kismet was silent for a long time. When he finally spoke, it was with a weary resigned voice. "I'm sure she'll take care of them."

Epilogue

The woman stood at the bow deck rail of the Norwegian coast guard vessel, statue-still and seemingly impervious to the cold as she stared out across the emptiness of the frozen white landscape. She did not dwell on the events which had transpired nearby just a few days earlier. Things had gone badly, but she did not consider it a failure. That was the thing about experiments; the goal wasn't necessarily to produce a set of desired outcomes, but rather to gather data with which to refine the experiment in the next iteration.

And she felt confident the next iteration would be the last.

Although his actions had very nearly cost her control of the organization, her eldest son's actions were consistent with his psychological profile. In the next phase, she would funnel his reckless ambition, focusing his supernova bright energy into a laser that would cut through the barrier between heaven and earth.

Her thoughts were already on that not-too-distant day.

It would take a few weeks to move the golden god-bodies from the wreckage of the seed vault, but that would be easy enough to do. The local authorities had already circulated the story that global warming in tandem with a power failure, had caused the permafrost inside the vault to melt, assuring the public that Vault Two, which contained almost a million seed samples had escaped unscathed. The repair effort would provide the perfect cover for recovery and removal of the contents of the Prometheus vault, and while she knew that many items had probably been damaged beyond repair, she only needed one viable god-body for completion of the grand design.

Once the anomalies—what her youngest had taken to calling "the elemental relics"—were recovered, she would have Ulrich use them to produce a supply of *ichor*, albeit in a more controlled fashion than before, which would permit Prometheus' scientists to begin harvesting genetic material.

And then?

Then she would be more than just the mother of a pair of demigods.

A voice intruded on her musings. "Ma'am?"

She turned and found one of the ship's officers, bundled up against the cold, standing beside her at the rail. The man had a pinched expression, as if he was the bearer of dire news.

They must have found him, she thought, hiding a smile.

She had told them what to expect, that this was a recovery operation. Ulrich would appear as dead to them, a drowning victim. She would have to move quickly to hide his resurrection from the crew.

Keeping her face expressionless, she faced the officer. "Have you found something?"

She was actually surprised it had taken them so long. The crew had been running search lanes using an array of instruments—towed sonar, magnetometers, even a remotely-operated undersea vehicle—for several hours already. The incident had occurred in shallow water, and she had expected quick results.

"No ma'am," the man said, and now she realized the real reason for his apprehension. "There's nothing here. Nothing at all."

"That's impossible. I saw him go into the ice right here. I saw with my own eyes."

The officer nodded patiently. "All the same, there's no trace of him. The captain requests that we expand the search area."

The woman frowned. She could understand how the body might have been carried away by currents and tides, but the relic should not have been affected by those forces.

Her mind raced with possibilities. Had Ulrich recovered on his own, escaping a watery grave with the relics in hand? It seemed unlikely, especially since she had placed the entire archipelago under intense surveillance almost from the moment she had witnessed her sons falling through the ice, but what other explanation could there be?

This iteration of the experiment was still ongoing, it seemed.

"Ma'am?" the officer asked again.

She blinked still pondering the significance of this development, then faced the officer. "Perhaps I did not see what I thought I saw," she said. "Tell the captain to call off the search and return to port. I have business elsewhere."

The End

ABOUT THE AUTHORS

David Wood is the USA Today bestselling author of the action-adventure series, The Dane Maddock Adventures, and many other works. He also writes fantasy under his David Debord pen name. When not writing, he hosts the Wood on Words podcast. David and his family live in Santa Fe, New Mexico. Visit him online at davidwoodweb.com.

Sean Ellis has authored and co-authored more than two dozen action-adventure novels, including the Nick Kismet adventures, the Jack Sigler/Chess Team series with Jeremy Robinson, and the Jade Ihara adventures with David Wood. He served with the Army National Guard in Afghanistan, and has a Bachelor of Science degree in Natural Resources Policy from Oregon State University. Sean is also a member of the International Thriller Writers organization. He currently resides in Arizona, where he divides his time between writing, adventure sports, and trying to figure out how to save the world. Learn more about Sean at seanellisauthor.com.